Warrior

English Dawn, Volume 2

Christopher Webster

Published by EKP, 2022.

WARRIOR

First edition. January 26, 2022.

Copyright © 2022 Christopher Webster.

ISBN: 979-8223455882

Written by Christopher Webster.

Table of Contents

The Empire Totters...1
The Way of the Warrior 9
Ordwyga 18
Waldere and Hildegund 25
A Garrulous Ferryman 34
Camalo..40
Kimo...43
Werinhard 45
Ekivrid 47
Hadawart...49
Patavrid 51
Gerwit 54
Randolf 57
Helmnod, Trogus and Tanastus 59
Mimming...62
In Armorica...69
Fate Versus Free Will...74
Sword of Albion..80
A Frail Old Man..84
The Empire Pleads for Help 88
Home at Last 97
The Advantage of No Hand 103
Marriage and Mimming 109
Being Boiled...114
Mission Impossible..121
On The March..126
The Empire Strikes Back 142
Ildico 155
Grand Alliance...158
Historical Note 165
Bibliography 174

This Heritage Edition is dedicated to all members of my family, in all branches, past, present and future, in all the four corners of the globe from Australia and the Philippines, to France and Canada, and various parts of the United Kingdom, including London, Oxfordshire and York, with a special mention of my children, Nicholas, Charlotte, James Christian and Christine Grace, and my grandchildren, Beatrice and Henry.

The Empire Totters

It was late afternoon, and the setting sun cast blood-red streaks across the horizon in a way that seemed to Eawa ominous rather than beautiful. "It's a bad omen," he said to his companion, Graf, "It looks like blood."

As if in response to this remark, a ragged old man with long grey hair and a straggling beard barred their way. He pointed a bony finger to the bloody sunset and wailed, "The last has come!"

"What are you talking about?" said Eawa.

"Rome's twelve centuries were augured by twelve vultures which ap-peared to Romulus when Rome was founded. Rome has had its twelve centuries and we are in its dying days!"

"We're not Romans, we're Goths!" said Eawa.

But the old man took no notice and continued his rant: "Attila is com-ing! It will be Vicinium all over again! Every man, woman and child slaughtered, and the city razed to the ground!"

"Not if we have anything to do with it," said Graf.

The old man cackled with hysterical laughter. "Can an old man like you fight the great Attila?"

"No but our army can!" said Eawa.

"Army, ha! What can a few hundred men do against the hordes of Asia!"

Eawa pushed the old man roughly aside. Prophets of doom are annoying enough, but when the disaster they prophesy is threatening to fall on your head, it's hard to ignore them. What is more, he and Graf, as counsellers to the king, carried the weighty responsibility of deciding what to do about it.

"There was no need to be so rough," said Graf. "The city's full of doomsayers nowadays – and for good reason: Attila has already destroyed dozens of cities and killed thousands of innocent citizens."

"There'll be no killing," said Eawa. "We must advise the king to sue for peace."

"I agree. We have no choice," but you know Ælfhere. He's a ditherer. By the time he's made his mind up, there'll be red in Burdigala as well as the sky.

Burdigala was their city, the capital of Gallia Aquitania. It was a former Roman city that had been taken by the Visigoths when the Romans left, and its infrastructure was still in good repair, including a circuit of walls that led some to believe that they could defy Attila.

They entered the council chamber, a large vaulted room in the old forum, to find King Ælfhere's thegns muttering softly amongst themselves, turning over every aspect of the situation, but finding no solution. A few wanted to try to hold out, but most had come to the same conclusion as Graf and Eawa, that negotiation was the best policy.

King Ælfhere began the council by asking Grimwald, his war-chief to sum up the situation. Grimwald, a grizzled veteran, rose to his feet, and coughed to clear his throat. He was more comfortable with fighting than speaking in public, but the situation make him almost eloquent:

"My lords, allow me to tell you what it is like when Attila takes a city. Have you heard of Vicinium? It is – or was – a major Roman city on the Danube. The governor decided to defend the city, but Attila smashed the aqueducts and the citizens drank water from the river and got sick or died. Food became scarce and the citizens were reduced to eating rats. When Attila finally breached the walls, he sacked the city for three days, and those who survived famine and disease were burned or tortured or raped, and all around the city lay dead bodies, bloody and naked, gnawed by rats and dogs."

Eawa rose to his feet, hoping to press the point: "That's the way Attila works – the fist and the glove. The fist is to crush anyone who opposes him with unbelievable cruelty; the glove is to treat with honour and respect all those who come to terms with him."

"And he has the sword!" continued Grimwald.

"What do you mean?" said Ælfhere.

"The Sword of Tengri – the sword of the Hunnic war god. It is said that, whosoever wields that sword, will rule the world!"

"Are you sure we can't hold out? The walls of Burdigala[1] are high; old Roman work. Nothing can bring them down," said the king – but he was clutching at a straw.

A new counsellor, by the name of Malrede, spoke in support. "My lord, you are so right about the strength of our defences, and I'm sure we all agree that we can hold out."

He was a young man of a most unwarrior-like appearance; thin, smooth-skinned, with a high-domed forehead, a scant beard, and dark brown, oily hair. He had clearly decided to make his way in politics, since he hadn't the physique – or perhaps the courage – required for a military career. His manner was as oily as his air. He seemed intent on pleasing everybody, and agreed with whatever anybody said, even when they expressed conflicting opinions.

Grimwald threw his arms up in despair. "My lord, with all respect. Please don't ask me to take on that monster! I have seen his army. It is numberless. There were so many men that all the earth groaned beneath their grinding feet; the air rang with the rattle of war-gear; it was like an iron forest flashing with light!"

Once again, fear of Attila inspired him with words that would not have disgraced a scop.

"So I propose that we sue for peace," said Eawa, intervening quickly before Malrede could get another word in.

"How?" said Ælfhere, hopefully.

"Isn't it the case that Gibicho convinced Attila to accept another hostage instead of Gunther?"

"That is true," said Grimwald, taking up the story. "He proposed a young nobleman called Hagen."

"Did he accept?" said Ælfhere, clutching at another straw.

"Yes," said the steward. "Hagen has a noble lineage; he is the last of the Nibelungs. Attila considered him a worthy substitute."

"I wonder who we could offer," mused Ælfhere, half to himself.

Malrede, eager to please the king, and to displace his most trusted counsellor, suggested, "What about Eawa, my lord? He is of noble lineage. Perhaps Attila would accept him." Then he turned to Eawa, and added in a conciliatory tone, "I mean it as a compliment, of course."

Eawa was unpleasantly surprised that this new counselor should put his ideas forward so boldly and was about to contradict him when he thought the better of it, and instead he bowed stiffly to show that he would accept his king's doom. After all, it was highly unlikely to happen, seeing as Waldere was of age.

There was a thoughtful silence in the chamber until Grimwald said, "Shall I go on, my lord?"

"Yes. Let's heard what happened in Burgundia."

Grimwald coughed to clear his voice and continued: "When King Hereric heard that Attila's army had crossed the Arar and the Rhone he sent ambassadors to negotiate a treaty. Attila said he would accept nothing less that 300 pounds of gold and his daughter as a hostage."

There were shocked mutterings in the chamber, and Ælfhere once again he thought of his son, particularly as he had made an arrangement with King Hereric that Hildegund and Waldere should marry when they were of age.

Grimwald continued: "At first, Hereric refused, but when his scouts reported that Attila was marching towards Cabillonum,[2] he had no choice but to accept his terms, so Hildegund was sent to Attila."

One of the lords gave a horrified gasp, and said to his companion in a low voice that was meant to be confidential, but which many overheard: "What! Hildegund! That beautiful innocent girl! She's Hereric's sole heir!"

Ælfhere saw where all this was leading: if a woman was acceptable as a hostage, there would be no persuading Attila to accept anyone else but his son. However, he refused to face up to it; if there had been a pile of sand in that chamber he would have buried his head in it. He brushed the obvious conclusion aside with the words, "There must be another way. Perhaps we can send to Rome for help."

"I agree," said Malrede. "Indeed, I would be honoured if you would allow me to write the letter."

Grimwald did not like to contradict his lord or Malrede, but he felt that he had to speak, so he coughed apologetically and began: "Rome's legions are a shadow of the past. They're a shambles of foederati, auxiliaries and poorly equipped legionaries."

Wise old Eawa gave a cynical laugh and said, "My lord, I have been to Rome, and I have seen it for myself. The citizens that used to man the legions are living dissipated lives: cheering on gladiators in the arena, bathing for hours each day in *balneae*[3] that are bigger than our burhs, gorging themselves at banquets that last for days, fornicating with other's wives or sex slaves, or common prostitutes..."

"Sound like a good life to me!" quipped Eofor, a young ne'er do well.

"It is – until Attila comes knocking on your door!" said Eawa, putting him in his place.

"Why can't we hold out?" asked Malrede "We have a large army – how many exactly, Grimwald?"

"300 in the here, 500 in the fyrd, more or less," he replied.

"More than enough to hold Burdigala, I should think!"

"Remember what Grimwald said about the size of Attila's army?" warned Graf.

"Yes – 'numberless' – but it was a scop's exaggeration."

"I am no scop!" said Grimwald forcefully. "I was just trying to make you understand the vast size of his army."

"Give us an exact number," said Malrede.

"They are too many to count, but it will be many thousands."

"Don't defenders always have an advantage?"

Grimwald considered this point, then replied, "Usually, yes, but Attila has learned the art of siege warfare from the Romans. Look what happened at Vicinium: he used siege towers and battering rams – and he'll do the same here."

Ælfhere was listening and taking note, but at the back of his mind was his reluctance to send his son as a hostage, and so he clutched at another straw: "Perhaps Attila will be satisfied with the conquest of two kingdoms and prefer to consolidate his gains rather than attack another."

"That is most likely, my lord," put in the obsequious Malrede,

A ripple of concern spread around the chamber. It was getting dark now, the sun had set and the lamps had been lit. Their feeble flames flickered in the draft, casting trembling shadows on the walls. Sometimes, when a stronger draft than usual swept through the chamber, the shadows seemed to move, as though they were already fighting the battle that they all dreaded.

Graf decided that it was time to speak up: "My lord, you have heard Grimwald. We cannot match the might of Attila, so we should sue for peace."

"I agree," said Eawa.

Many voices were raised in support, but Ælfhere clung on to the hope that Attila might not venture so far west: "We will wait and see," he said, rising to signal that the meeting was over before any objections could be raised.

Only a few days later, scouts reported that Attila was on the move and was heading west, but when his lords pressed the idea of a treaty, Ælfhere refused to listen, saying only, "Perhaps he will turn north."

Needless to say, Malrede agreed with him.

Wishful thinking is one thing, but hard facts are another, and they hit Ælfhere in the face when, not long after, the lookout, seeing a cloud of dust, cried: "Attila is coming!"

Ælfhere gave the order to close the gates and man the walls, But Grimwald hesitated. "You're not thinking of trying to hold out, are you?" He spoke more boldly than before because his fear of Attila was greater than his fear of offending his lord. "My lord, remember Vicinium. Burdigala will end up the same – an apocalypse of dead bodies rabaged by wolves!"

Ælfhere, fearing that he and his beloved son, Waldere, might end up among those wolf-ravaged bodies, finally admitted that he had no choice but to make terms. He still clung to the hope that Attila would accept Eawa as a hostage instead of his son, but Attila wouldn't hear of it. Waldere was of age, so it was him or nothing. As usual, Malrede agreed with the king in everything, despite his numerous changes of mind.

Later that day, Ælfhere himself led his ambassadors to Attila's camp with his son and wagonloads of tribute – 300 pounds of gold in goods and chattels. He trembled at the thought of meeting this terrifying man face to face. He had heard that he was a devil incarnate, a *draugur*,[4] a Loki come to Middle-Earth, but was surprised to find a man of short of stature, with a broad chest and a large head, with a sprinkling of grey in his hair and beard. Only his small eyes, flat nose and swarthy complexion made him seem somewhat sinister, but his courteous manner soon dispelled that impression. Indeed, Attila behaved more like a man receiving honoured guests than a conqueror receiving the representatives of a subject nation. He even went so far as to shake Ælfhere by the hand and say: "I would rather come to terms with my opponents, if they are willing, than wage war. We Huns prefer peace!"

Ælfhere was stricken by the irony of this remark from the man who had ravaged half the world, but schooled himself to keep a straight face. Then he remembered Eawa's words about the first and the glove – this was the glove. However, Eawa was not there; Malrede, who was, said afterwards, "You handled it well, my lord. Attila was much impressed by you. I'm sure that he has treated no other king with such courtesy."

Next day, Attila raised the siege and returned to Pannonia with a veritable wagon train of booty – the wealth of three kingdoms: Francia, Burgundia and Aquitania, along with guarantees of further tribute, and three hostages: Hagen, Hildegund and Waldere.

The Way of the Warrior

The glove treatment continued in Pannonia. Waldere had wondered how they would be accommodated. Would it be a prison or a palace? He guessed that it would be something in between, but it turned out to be a palace – Attila's palace; not that Attila believed luxury. His 'palace' was nothing more than a large and well-built wooden hall, with a planked floor and simple furnishings, but such as it was Hagen, Hildegund and Waldere had the freedom of it. They found themselves treated as honoured guests rather than hostages, indeed, more than honoured guests, for Attila fostered them like a father, raising them as his own. He asked his queen, Ospirin, to care for the girl and teach her womanly ways and courtly manners, adding that he himself would instruct Waldere and Hagen in the martial arts.

Waldere and Hagen had hardly got settled in their new home when Attila roused them one morning before first light, and took them to a nearby stream. It was early March, and the water was ice cold, but Attila insisted that they lay in it. When Hagen asked him what it was all about he simply replied, "It will toughen you up."

So they took off their clothes and lay down in the stream, their bodies shivering and their teeth chattering. After a less than a minute, Waldere had had enough, and started to climb out.

"Not yet!" said Attila. "You've only just got started."

After about 10 minutes, he relented and let them get out and get dried. They were white-skinned and shivering, hopping around like lame dogs, while rubbing themselves vigorously with towels to get warm and dry.

"Now I'll show you how it should be done!" said Attila, stripping himself and getting into the stream. He lay there as though it had been the warmest bed of comfortable feather down in Pannonia. He even had a smile on his face.

"You must show contempt for pain, hardship and danger! That way, men will respect you," he explained. "Tomorrow, I will expect you to show the same indifference."

Next morning, they slid into the water and tried not to shiver, but it was not easy, and Waldere had to grit his teeth to do it. He was still a long way from the comfortable smile that Attila affected.

After their morning bath, Attila started them on wrestling. "Wrestling is the queen of martial arts," he said. "It teaches balance, power and control. When you have mastered wrestling, you can choose whether to tackle an opponent on your feet or on the ground, and anyone who comes to hand-grips with you will get the worst it. Now, both of you together – attack me!"

Hagan, still a little angry from his ice-cold soaking, charged at Attila head on. As soon as Hagen was within reach, Attila hooked his nearest arm with both hands, and fell backwards, forcing Hagen's momentum to flip him over his head. Waldere was close behind him, but Attila sidestepped, put his head under Waldere's shoulder, lifted him up, and dropped him tailbone-first on his knee. Waldere rolled away in agony. Attila laughed.

"Now," said Attila, "we'll start from the beginning. I'm going to teach you the double leg takedown."

He demonstrated the moves, then told the two young men to practice on each other.

After what seemed a long morning, they went back to Attila's hall, only to find that the day had hardly begun.

"We will take refreshment – just bread and water – gourmandising is weakening – then we shall see what can be done with a sword."

The youths found that the Hunnic sword was different to the Nordic sword with which they were familiar. Called the *urepos*, it was a little over three feet long, straight and narrow, with a very short quillion, offering little hand protection. It was lighter than the swords that they were used to, seeming almost flimsy by comparison, though the light weight made it more lively in use. Waldere, who fancied himself as something of a swordsman, looked at his urepos doubtfully – and there was something else that was troubling him: "We're not going to practice with sharp weapons are we?"

Attila laughed, "Only babies play with wooden swords," though he knew full well that Roman legionaries practiced with weighted wooden swords, "and anyway, a bit of blood will toughen you up."

Waldere was just about to protest when Attila added, "Don't worry, we'll wear armour." With these words he signalled to his servants to help them arm themselves. Like the swords, the armour was also different to the ring-mail byrnie to which the youths were accustomed. It was lamellar armour made up of a series of metal plates stitched together; lighter than the byrnie, but perhaps less protective. The helmet was not so different to the ones he was used to. It was conical with a horsehair plume, and had a nasal and a long mail aventail The shield was much smaller than any he had used, being designed for use by horse archers.

When they were armed, Attila said again, "Attack me – one at a time this time. Waldere you go first."

Waldere was wary of Attila now, and had little doubt what the outcome would be. Nevertheless, he believed himself to be a good swordsman, and was determined to give a good account of himself. He approached Attila with his sword in the guard position, expecting that they would circle around each other thrusting and blocking until one of them saw a gap and made the mighty stroke that would defeat their opponent. But Attila began to dance round him with dozens of cuts that were so rapid his sword was nothing but a blur – a technique well suited to the light urepos.

Waldere blocked as well as he could, but when your opponent's sword is a blur, it's hard to know where to block, and more and more cuts fell on his armour. The lamellar cuirass that Attila had given him was not as good as his trusty ring-mail byrnie, but good enough to protect him from Attila's swordstrokes, which were not intended to wound or kill, only to train. It ended when Attila's sword flashed suddenly in front of his face.

"If this had been a real fight, your throat would be gushing blood by now!" said Attila, stepping back. "Now, Hagen. It's your turn."

Hagen's plight was much the same: Attila danced around him and in moments his urepos was at his throat.

After the demonstration, Attila began to teach the two youths the techniques of the urepos, beginning with the *moulinet*, the spinning of the sword, and continuing with a range of cuts, and techniques to parry them.

In the afternoon it was horse riding. Their mounts were the small and sturdy *aduu*, or Mongol horse. Waldere was confused by the stirrups, which he had never seen before, but soon found that they gave him a secure seat and better control of the horse.

"We Huns grow up on horseback," said Attila, "so that by the time we are men, they feel like part of our own bodies. If you are to fight with us, you must feel the same."

He rode them up and down and round and round teaching them to control the horse with their knees so that their arms were free for fighting – and that led them to the last lesson of the day – the use of the recurved bow. The bows were much smaller than any bow that Waldere had used before, but almost as strong due to their composite construction of bamboo, horn and sinew, bound together with animal glue. However, both he and Hagen found it almost impossible to do much with the bow on horseback. Attila told them to ride past a tree and try to put an arrow into it, but their arrows went wide of the mark. There was another problem about the bow. Nordic warriors regard the bow as a cowardly weapon which you can use kill your opponent without manfully coming to grips with him. So though the two youths tried their best, their heart wasn't in it.

Attila knew nothing of this; to a Hun the bow is the most important weapon, and has to feel as much a part of him as his horse does. So he just laughed at their feeble efforts, and demonstrated how it should be done. He galloped past the tree at a breakneck pace and managed to put three arrows in the centre of the trunk, one as he approached, one as he passed, and the third by twisting round in his saddle and shooting behind him.

"We'll work on it!" he said with his usual hearty laugh. "But that's enough for today. Tomorrow, after a refreshing morning bath…" he laughed even more at the thought of how they'd shivered that morning, "we will make a start on polearms, the staff, the spear, the glaive – but now it's time to raise the flowing blow!"

But even over the wine bowl, Attila was still teaching them. Indeed, that was the time when they studied the most important of all the martial arts: strategy. They would play *tafl*, sometimes Waldere against Hagen, sometimes Attila against both of them, and as they played he would draw lessons from the game:

"All warfare is based on deception."

"Appear weak when you are strong, strong when you are weak."

"Attack your enemy where he is unprepared."

After the morning bath, Attila gave each of the youths a staff. "A spear is a staff with a point, and we can use a staff to learn the guards. Let me show you."

Attila demonstrated the three main guards, the high guard, the middle guard and the low guard, and how each could be used as the starting point for an attack. He demonstrated them in use, by, once again, asking the youths to attack him. "If either of you can score one strike on my body, I'll spare you the morning bath tomorrow!" But, of course, they couldn't get anywhere near him. Whichever way they thrust and swung, he had a guard to block them; many more than the three main guards he had shown them. Even when the youths attacked together, he held them off, sometimes with the long end of his staff, and sometimes with the rear quarter behind his right hand. He ended the bout by grabbing Waldere's staff and throwing it to the ground. Waldere replied by trying to grab Attila's staff, but Attila twisted it around his thumb, making him shout with pain and let go. "I'll teach you that move," he said, "it is one of four defences if your opponent tries to grab your staff or spear. He taught them the four moves, then said, "Now practice together, and this afternoon we will see what can be done with spears."

Attila began the afternoon session by throwing a spear at the same tree that he had used as a target for arrows. At a distance of 15 paces, it hit the trunk dead centre. "If you can learn to throw a spear like that, you won't need the guards we learned this morning. Now you try."

They both missed, 15 paces being a longer range than they were used to. "Try again," said Attila, and this time hold your spears parallel to the ground and follow through." They did as he advised and continued for the rest of the afternoon, while Attila watched and gave advice.

Next day, they practices with the staffs again. This time they had to throw the staffs at each other like spears and practice dodging them.

"You have to dance like a maiden at a wedding!" laughed Attila. "Watch and dance! That's the secret!"

And so their training continued: the morning bath in the mountain stream followed by one martial art after another, every day, without a break month after month, year after year.

Waldere proved an adept at all the marshal arts; he was strong, intelligent and had quick reactions, Hagen was not far behind him, so as soon as they had mastered the horse and the bow, Attila invited them to take part in his campaigns. Before long, Waldere and Hagen were better than most of his men, and Attila, who valued merit above all else, put them in charge of his army, with Waldere in the honoured position of *ordwyga* (general), despite the fact that they were not Huns. Indeed, he treated them like his own sons.

Hildegund also won Ospirin's good will by her honesty and her industry. At first, Ospirin thought she was one of those empty-headed blonde beauties, because she had so little to say for herself. That was because she was struggling with the language, which is highly inflected and difficult to learn. While she was learning, she said little, but her bright, intelligent eyes were darting everywhere, looking and learning, and when she did speak, her words showed her common sense – wisdom, even.

Ospirin taught her everything a Hunnic lady should know: how to manage a household, how to entertain guests courteously, and to understand the many customs that governed daily life. Not that she always agreed with them.

"When you marry you will have your own household to manage," said Ospirin, "that's why you need to learn these things."

"It is the same in Burgundia," said Hildegund.

"And you will be expected to please your husband in every way."

"Will he be expected to please me?"

"It is not like that among the Huns. You will be, as it were, his handmaid."

"Won't we have maids and thralls?"

"Yes, but you will be his very special handmaid. You must obey his every whim without question."

"Are Hunnic women just servants then?"

"In particular, you must satisfy his manly needs – do you understand me?"

Hildegund understood, but did not like the idea. "What if I am not in the mood?"

"Your moods have nothing to do with it. You must satisfy him, or he will seek his pleasure with another wife."

"Another wife? What do you mean?"

"Surely you have seen that, among the Huns, it is the custom for a man to have more than one wife."

"It is not like that in Burgundia!"

"You are not in Burgundia. You are a Hunnic woman now and must behave like one."

Hildegund didn't think much of the way the Huns treated their women, but she was wise enough to bow her head meekly and appear to accept it. Like Waldere and Hagen, she was surprised at the way she had been welcomed. She was just a hostage, after all, and had expected to be treated like a prisoner – a high class prisoner, of course, with a comfortable cell and good food – but to be treated like an adopted daughter was beyond all expectations, and she was determined to make the most of it, even when Ospirin threw another obstacle in the way of her happiness:

"Of course, Attila and I will choose your husband."

"But I am promised to Waldere!"

Ospirin gave a dismissive laugh. "That was in another life. You are both Huns now, and Attila and I know what is best for each of you.

I have someone in mind for Waldere, though I'm not sure what we're going to do with you just yet."

Hildegund wanted to jump up, pout, stamp her feet, and make a pretty little tantrum, just as she would have done back in Burgundia, but she knew it would do no good. The best plan, as always, was to appear to agree, and keep in Ospirin's good graces. However, she decided that she must speak to Waldere about it.

Her restraint paid off, because Attila and Ospirin formed such a high opinion of her that she was asked to be Attila's steward and to take care of all his treasure – a huge responsibility. As a token of this she carried a large key which hung from her waistband – the key to the Attila's treasury. Beside it was a token of protection which she brought from Burgundy, and which she was allowed to keep: a small seax, with a single-edged blade about six inches long. The sheath was ornamented with jewels, but the blade was razor sharp – and she knew how to use it.

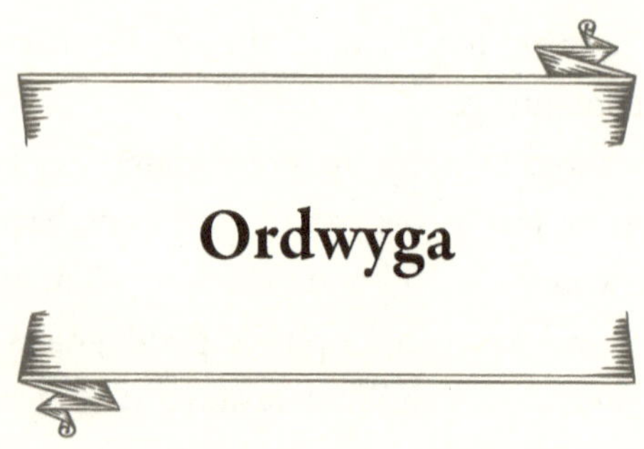

Ordwyga

Gebicho died and Gunther succeeded him, but he was not the man his father was. He was courageous to the point of recklessness, but a fool in the council chamber. He had no idea of diplomacy, either with allies or enemies, or even in his own court. He had surrounded himself with flatterers, the most obsequious of whom was a noble called Herigend, who (in return for gifts of land and gold) told Gunther what he wanted to hear. Any of the nobles who spoke against his whims found themselves out in the cold – sometimes literally. Indeed, a noble called Tarp, Gebicho's oldest and most trusted counsellor, after a disagreement about the treaty with Attila, found himself stripped of his position and most of his lands, leaving him with only a tumble-down mead-hall in a remote part of Francia.

"We've not seen Attila for donkey's years," Gunther said at the next meeting. "He's finished, I tell you, and what's more, I've been building up a mighty army. It is now the biggest army that Francia has ever seen. So, my lords, I propose that we tear up the treaty with Attila and put those wagon loads of tribute to better use."

His nobles knew what Gunther was thinking of: first and foremost, more money for the army, his pet project, but also for his pleasures: a new hall, a stud of finest Arabian horses, wine from Falernia, spices from Carthage, and his latest idea, a dowry large enough to tempt the king of the Heathobards to offer him his daughter's hand in marriage. Freawaru was reputed to be a beauty, fair of face and full of figure, though Gunther valued the alliance more than the woman, as it was part of Herigend's scheme to attack Frisia from both sides now that it had been weakened by the feud with the Half-Danes.

It was a mad idea, as the Franks were more likely to be crushed by Attila than be able to form an empire of their own, but after the demotion of Tarp, nobody dared to say anything. Only one naïve young man by the name of Leofric spoke up, though tentatively, "My lord, forgive me if I express my fears, but what shall we do if Attila comes seeking reprisals?"

Gunther gave a dismissive laugh. "Fight him, of course. As I said, our army is now the biggest army that Francia has ever seen, and with the tribute money we save we can hire mercenaries – and there is no shortage of those, these days. We can take our pick: Angles, Saxons, Eotens, Geats, Goths...I could go on. Another thing is that I am hoping to build an alliance with Aetius."

"Those are good plans," my lord, said Herigend quickly, before anyone could speak in support of the doubter. "Aetius is building a legion to fight Attila, and with him on our side, and our own mighty army, the Hun will run away like a kicked dog!"

Gunther's sycophants cheered in support, and Leofric was silenced, though he couldn't help thinking that there would soon be a hell of a lot of kicked dogs, and they wouldn't be Huns!

Hagen was horrified when he heard the news that Gunther had broken the treaty. As Attila's hostage he was the one who would have to pay for it – and he knew too well Attila's rapid changes of mood from the fist to the glove – or in this case, the other way round. Since the day he had been taken as a hostage, Attila had treated him with the utmost courteousness, and latterly had treated him like a son – but had not Attila killed his own brother? – and might he not turn against his adopted son and have him killed also?

"I must go," he said to Waldere that night, explaining his reasons.

"Will you go back to Francia?"

Hagen gave a bitter snort. "What, and have Attila at my back? – for you can be sure that the Franks are in for his fist and his boot. You know what Attila is like when a city resists him – he stamps on it, like an angry boy crushing a beetle: everything is destroyed, no-one is spared. No. I'm going as far away from him as possible. I'll head south, perhaps to Worms – but don't breath a word of it!"

Next morning he was gone, and when Attila found out, he exploded in a storm of anger. "After all I did for that boy! If I ever get my hands on him..." he smashed his right fist into his left palm which finished his sentence more eloquently than any words could do. Then he snarled, with a look like a ravening wolf: "In the meantime, his people in Francia will pay the price! I'll make an example of them! I'll wipe them off the face of the earth! Not one man, woman or child will be left alive! – That will be a lesson to any other treaty-breakers!"

Ospirin, who knew his moods, tried to console him. "Cheer up, my love. You still have Waldere, and he's the better man of the two. But listen to my advice for once: beware, lest Waldere follow him. Why don't you offer him a wife, a woman of the Huns, someone who will tempt his fancy? What about Hildaz? She's only 15, but has a woman's body, with a bosom that a man would want to fondle all night. She has a pretty face too – what eyes! Like almonds, and what lips! Full, pouting – he'll never stop kissing her! Her hips, too, suggest that she'll pop out his heirs as fast as he can pump in the seed. What man could resist her? Also, you should shower him with riches: a hall, retainers and land, rings of twisted gold, gems from the Brisingamen hoard. Let's face it, my love, you could give him a mountain of treasure and you'd never miss it, so why not do it and keep him faithful?"

Ospirin's plan pleased Attila and he acted on it immediately. He sent for Waldere and offered him Hildaz and rich rewards, but Waldere could only refuse, despite his appreciation of the nubile Hildaz. Above all, because he was promised to Hildegund, but also because he wanted to keep his independence. He knew that Attila would crush Francia, and he wanted no part of it. After all, the Franks and the Burgundians were old allies. Indeed, he had thoughts of following Hagen's example and making a run for it. Only the thought of Hildegund held him back. He couldn't leave her alone in Pannonia – so he made excuses: "I thank you, lord, for offering these things, but if I take a wife I will be distracted from doing my duty: building homes, instead of battling your enemies; ploughing fields, instead of pillaging their lands; fondling the fair Hildaz instead of fighting your foes. You taught me that whoever can stand pain wins the respect of your warriors, but whoever tastes pleasure can take less pain. Therefore I beg you, allow me live my life alone. That way, if you send for me in the middle of the night I shall serve you without fear for my family's welfare; in war, no doubts will weaken me, nor wife or sons make me long for home and tempt me to desert. Best of fathers, bravest of leaders, please do not make me a married man!"

Perhaps Waldere should have taken up the study of rhetoric and become a lawyer in Rome, for he had found just the right arguments to convince Attila, who left him feeling quite certain that the loyal Waldere would never leave his service.

Next day, as Waldere had feared, he was put in charge of the reprisals on Francia – but what could he do? He had decided to stay for Hildegund's sake in the full knowledge that he would be given this unpleasant task. So he tried to forget that the Franks and the Aquitani were allies, and made his preparations in the usual way. He encouraged his warriors and gave them heart, reminding them of previous triumphs and promising them that they would bring the Franks to heel as easily as if they were disobedient dogs.

They marched to Francia, bringing a range of siege engines, for despite his confident speech, Waldere was worried about the high walls of the old Roman city, as his army consisted of horse archers and fought best in the open. Imagine his surprise and relief when he saw a cloud of dust on the horizon and discovered that the Franks were marching to meet him. What fool had ordered that? They had thrown away their only advantage and played into their enemy's hands!

The armies stopped just outside bowshot and heralds were sent to parlay. Waldere, hating to fight with former friends, had decided to disobey Attila by giving Gunther a chance to back down and restore the treaty. But the over-confident and badly-counselled Gunther wouldn't hear of it, and as soon as the heralds had returned to their lines, gave the order to attack.

Then a clamour arose: the cries of men, the wail of warhorns, the whinnying of horses. Then flew the arrows, the adders of war, followed by spears, the serpents of death. When the spears were spent, each Frank drew his sword, and sheltering behind his bull-hide, shield struck for his home, his hearth and his hoard (if he was lucky enough to have one).

Waldere signalled to his men to begin their usual tactic, and soon they were galloping like furies, not towards, but across the van of the Franks. Then, with lighting speed, and with few horseman to oppose them, they rode around the flanks of their enemy, and galloped across their rear. They went round and round in a vortex, confusing to the Franks because they had no idea where their enemy would strike next. If they raised their bull-hide shields to the front, the Huns were at their back, if they turned to face them, they were at the left side or the right side, showering them with arrows from their powerful recurved bows.

Gunther's 'mighty army' floundered under the onslaught, then broke and bolted, but the Huns pursued them relentlessly and hacked them down without mercy. Those that could, fled to the city, and waved white flags of surrender from the gatehouse. Attila had ordered that every man, woman and child be put to the sword and the city razed to the ground, but Waldere, partly because of his friendship with Hagen, and partly in common humanity, could not countenance this, and ordered that the city be spared on condition that double the tribute was paid, and that Gunther himself should be the hostage, while a Hun puppet king ruled in his place.

As it happened, Attila was more than satisfied with the destruction of the Frankish army, the wagonloads of tribute, and his royal hostage, and welcomed his *ordwyga* with open arms and the promise of a great rewards to celebrate his victory: gold, jewels, land, horses, slaves – and the nubile Hildaz – though Waldere still refused her.

So Ospirin decided to take the matter of Hildaz into her own hands. "My lord," she said to Attila, "Waldere now has all the wealth we spoke of. If only we could persuade him to take Hildaz, he would be settled for life."

"He has refused her," said Attila, "and has given good reasons. He said he would serve me better in battle without the distraction of a wife – and you see the result!"

"Nevertheless, we should try again. Leave it to me."

Later that day, Ospirin sent for Waldere to attend her in the women's' quarter. Men, other than the great lord himself, were not usually allowed in there, so she sent her personal bodyguard to escort him.

As soon as he walked through the door, Waldere saw it; the show that Ospirin had prepared for him: there, at the far end of the room, behind a curtain of transparent gauze, Hildaz was taking a bath. Ospirin made a pretence of surprise: "Oh, Waldere! I wasn't expecting you just yet! Hildaz has not finished her bath."

Waldere muttered an apology and turned to go, but she took his arm and turned him back. "But now that you are here, why not take a good look and see what you are turning down. Girls!"

At her call, the thralls dropped the curtain and Hildaz, who stood up as if in surprise, was revealed in all her naked glory. She had long black hair that fell to her buttocks. It was wet and clung to her body, accentuating her curves. Her eyes were black too, exciting and exotic because of their almond shape, accentuated by a touch of kohl. Her skin was nothing like the sallow dun of Hunnic menfolk, but was a beautiful honey-gold, glistening now with the water that streamed down it. Her body was unusually shapely for one of her race, with breasts which were large and full, but high and firm, with large brown nipples that seemed to stare at him invitingly – two delicious handfuls! Her belly was sleek and flat, and ornamented by a jewel in her bellybutton. Her hips were broad, promising easy childbearing, and her legs long and elegant, more so than was usual with Hunnic women.

"Just say the word and she is yours," whispered Ospirin.

Waldere was sorely tempted. He had just won honour and great wealth; all that was lacking was a wife. But he understood the consequences: he would then be one of them; he would be a Hun.

Ospirin continued to urge him: "Isn't she lovely? You can take her now, on the bed in the next room, as long as you promise to marry her as soon as I can arrange it."

Hildaz stepped out of the bath and reached for a towel. As she did so, her whole body quivered subtly; ripples of flesh from bosom to bottom, and as she stooped, those breasts dipped, displaying them in all their fullness. She turned to pick up a jar of olive oil, displaying her other mounds, full and firm and inviting the touch. Indeed, her movements were almost a dance, and a most seductive dance it was. But Ospirin had overplayed her hand: Waldere suddenly saw it for what it was: a pre-planned show in which every movement had been choreographed beforehand, and once he was on that bed with her, he was snared! That thought dampened his ardour, and with a slight bow and a few diplomatic words, he left Ospirin wondering what she had done wrong.

Waldere and Hildegund

Waldere was trembling as he hurried away. It had been a close call: Hildaz! A high hall among the Huns! Honour! Riches! What more could a man want? The answer was simple: Hildegund! Honour to his father, Ælfhere, and his people, the Aquitani. As for riches, only fat burghers worried about them. If you lived a life of honour, riches would follow, just as riches had followed his successful campaign against the Franks.

He felt that he couldn't face his lord's questions about Hildaz, or take part in another rollicking celebration in the hall, so he made his way to a private chamber at the back of Attila's hall – and there was the woman he had been thinking about – Hildegund, golden haired, gracious, sitting alone. His heart leapt at the sight of her. Her golden hair being worth more to him than all the gold that Attila had just heaped on him, or than Hildaz' ebony waterfall. He gave her greeting, threw himself down on a settle and said, "Bring me some wine, I am worn out!"

So she filled a goblet and gave it to Waldere, who drained the cup and handed it back to her with a kiss, holding her hand at the same time. She looked at him and he looked at her, lost in the beauty of her sky-blue eyes, so different from the black blankness he saw in Hildaz'. That look said it all, and both of them knew that their betrothal had been acted out in that exchange.

With a heartfelt sigh, Waldere spoke the thoughts that had been in his heart for a long time, "We have both endured exile so long, knowing full well what our parents arranged. How much longer must we hide our love?"

Hildegund's answer was just as heartfelt: "It is not easy, living as we do – but I heard that Attila had other plans for you."

Waldere laughed. "He has – Hildaz is her name! As pretty a piece of Hunnic womanhood as you could find!"

Hildegund frowned and made a pout. Waldere kissed it. "But nothing compared to you – a fecund body but an empty head!"

He kissed her again, and for a long time they sat together, their arms around each other, until Waldere, who had been thoughtful, said, "I hate this exile, especially now that Hagen has gone. Even worse is the dishonour I feel at making war on his people, so I'm thinking of doing what he did – getting out of here! I would have gone before, but didn't want to leave you behind."

Tears of gratitude sprang into Hildegund's eyes, then, brushing away her tears, she looked up boldly. "Let's go! I hate this place! The queen is good to me, but, I am sick of her lessons in womanliness! Why should I learn needlework? Don't we have bond slaves for that? – and courtly manners. I know they're important, but I'd rather be with you in the open air!"

"What? Learning to fight?"

"Why not?"

"But you are a woman."

"I have heard that women fight too, what do they call them – Amazons, scyldmædens..."

Waldere knew that Hildegund was a strong woman – she had to be to survive the suffering of her life of a hostage, but the idea of her wielding sword and spear was too much for him. "Do you really want to be a scyldmæden?" he said.

She laughed her musical laugh. "Not really! Though I know how to use this!" She pulled her seax half out of its sheath then pushed it back again. "Father taught me. He said I should use it to defend my honour."

"So you are a scyldmæden after all!"

"Not really. I am a woman and will fight in a woman's way."

"What's that?"

"I'll use manipulation to get what I want."

"And what do you want?"

"You!"

That was an invitation to another round of hugging and kissing. It was a revelation to Waldere that such tender hand-grips could be more thrilling than wrestling. Hildegund liked it too, but she had not forgotten the drift of their conversation, and after one more deep draught of the wine of love, she said in a voice still husky with emotion, "Let's do it!"

Waldere was shocked. "We can't do it here. Somebody might come in!"

She smacked him playfully and said, with a girlish laugh, "No, not that! You know that I must keep my jewel until we are married. What I meant was – let's get away!"

Waldere laughed with her, then racked his brain to think of a plan. He got up and paced up and down the chamber, as restless as the thoughts in his mind. Then an idea came to him that was so daring he was afraid to say it out loud. Instead, he sat down again and leaned towards Hildegund as though he was going to kiss her, but his mouth went to her ear instead of her lips. Hildegund sighed with pleasure, expecting an amorous nibble, but instead he whispered his plan: "You are the guardian of the king's treasure-hoard. I want you to take that wondrous war-shirt, worked by Weland, which Attila took from my father as part of the tribute, and also *Mimming*, that far-famed sword. Then take as much gold as you can pack into two coffers. We'll also need hooks for fishing and bird-lime to catch birds, because we'll have to keep away from people and all we'll have to eat is what we can catch."

"I'll do it," said Hildegund, "but how can we get out of this place without being noticed?"

Waldere frowned. "That won't be easy with two horses laden with Attila's treasures!"

Hildegund jumped up suddenly, "I'll tell you how!" she began in an excited voice. Then, realising she was speaking too loudly, carried on in a whisper: "There'll be a feast to celebrate your victory, so let's make sure that the king and his lords drown themselves in a river of drink. Meanwhile, you must drink moderately, and when they all are befuddled with wine we'll sneak away."

So, after another round of that least martial of all the arts, lovemaking, they went their separate ways to make preparations. Hildegund went to the treasury to find the things that Waldere wanted, while he, taking over from Attila's steward, ordered all the food and wine, making sure that the food was the driest and saltiest, and that the wine was the sweetest and strongest. He particularly emphasised the latter point to the merchant, who gave him a sample, saying with a laugh, "This one will knock a man down sooner than your right hand!"

It is the custom among the Huns that the queen herself, helped by her handmaidens, serves the first round of drinks. Hildegund was among them, and made sure that each man's goblet was filled to the brim. The wine was sweetened with added spices, tempting the guests to drink deeply and long. The dry, salty food was another inducement to keep drinking.

When the first round of drinks was barely begun, Waldere proposed another. First he topped up Attila's goblet, and then moved along the table refilling the goblets of his lords. Attila protested at this, "Sit down, Waldere! This feast is in your honour. It is I who should pour a drink for you!" But as soon as Attila's head was turned, Waldere poured the drink on the floor behind him.

When the final course was finished, Attila rose and proposed a toast: "Let's drink to the hero of the day – Waldere!"

"Waldere!" the guests responded, rising and raising their goblets.

Waldere answered with a toast of his own: "Our lord, Attila, the great conqueror, made it possible! Here's to Attila!"

"Attila!"

"And to his army!"

"The army!"

Hildegund, seeing what Waldere was trying to do, thought of another toast:

"And to our queen, Ospirin!"

"Ospirin!"

Each toast meant a gulp from the goblet, so Waldere racked his brains to think of more: "To future victories!"

"Future victories!"

"To the downfall of the Empire!"

"The downfall of the Empire!"

"And Attila's new empire!"

"Attila's new empire!"

"Attila! The ruler of the world!"

By now, the wine was beginning to take its toll on some of the guests, as their responses showed: "Athilla, the ruler oth the worlth!"

But there were hard fighting, hard drinking warriors among them who would need a lot more than a few toasts to knock them down. So Waldere proposed that it was time for the ladies to withdraw, as was the custom, and Attila gave the word. At the same time, the tables were removed, and the banquet turned into a drink-fest. Waldere was determined to keep the drinking going at a fast pace, and even went so far as to say to Attila, "I beg that your grace give a good example in making merry!" Attila replied with a hearty laugh and said to his retainers, "This is the way, my lords!" after which he drained his goblet in one deep draught and ordered his lords to do likewise.

At Waldere's behest the servants served more wine immediately, giving the lords full bowls and taking them back empty. The lords enjoyed drinking for its own sake, but, as their lord had desired it, they drank more than usual, and even competed in drinking. Soon the drunkard was lord of the feast: eloquent speechmakers spluttered their words, good friends fell out and quarreled, and well-muscled warriors tottered like old men.

In this way, Waldere kept the drinking going all night, holding back those who wanted to go, until one by one, sleep overcame them and they slipped to the ground. Then, even if he'd set the place on fire, there was no-one awake to know what was happening.

When he saw them all lying there snoring noisily, he went to find his woman and asked her to bring what she had prepared, then went to get his favourite horse, whom he had called *Lion* on account of his courage. When he had saddled *Lion*, he hung on the gold-filled coffers like saddlebags, added a pack of modest provisions and gave the reins into Hildegund's hands. Then he armed himself, but in the old style, as a Visigoth, not as a Hun. Instead of the lamellar cuirass that Attila had given him, he wore the heirloom byrnie, that was once Ælfhere's, and should have been his, but which had been given to Attila in tribute. He would have liked to worn a broadsword, but the only one of any worth was the famed heirloom, *Mimming*, which he was loth to put to common use in case the edges were notched. So instead he strapped on his urepos, which hung from two straps at an angle so as to be quick on the draw, and on his right side his Hunnic single-edged short sword, the *akinakes*, which was not so very different from the Nordic seax. He wore his Hunnic helmet, as none other was available, and which, apart from the horsehair plume, was similar to the helmets worn by the Aquitani. His armour was completed by a stiff skirt of boiled leather and horn splints bound around his calves. He had little use for the small Hunnic shield, but luckily had found a large round Nordic shield which had been captured from the Franks. The

Visigoths prefer to fight on foot, and a large shield is an essential part of their equipment. Despite all his training with Attila, Waldere never felt comfortable on a horse, preferring the Visigoth custom of riding to battle and dismounting to fight. He had never taken to archery, either, and decided that bow and arrows would be unnecessary weight, especially as he had to carry two spears, one to throw, the other to fight with if he was unable to retrieve the first one.

The arming complete, they set off on their journey. Hildegund walked ahead leading the horse with a hazel-rod in her hand, ready to hook fish, for Waldere was burdened with armour, fearing that he might need to fight at any moment. They travelled all night, but when the world-candle rose above the horizon, they left the road and hid in the forest. Dread wore them down, darkened their mood, and the woman shuddered and shook with fear at every whisper of the windy breeze, scared by birds or the snapping of twigs.

"I thought you wanted an outdoor life!" said Waldere, half-joking.

"I did, but not while being pursued by Hunnish hordes!"

"Where is the scyldmæden in you?"

"Scyldmæden?"

"You know what I mean."

"She's there, but she's still getting used to it."

"Then don't be frightened of every little thing."

She gave a wan smile and promised to be brave, and she was: her loathing of exile and of being patronised by Ospirin, gave her the courage to go on.

The following day Waldere's friends went to find him and thank him for the feast. Attila, his head throbbing with a hangover, also wanted to see him, but his attendants answered that Waldere was nowhere to be found. He laughed and answered lightly: "Leave him to sleep – he needs it after all that drinking!"

But Ospirin, missing Hildegund's help to dress, and being unable to find her anywhere, realised what had happened. She went to Attila and told him the bad news: "The Demon Drink has destroyed the Huns!"

"What are you on about?" growled Attila. "The men deserve a banquet after a battle!"

"I warned you, my lord, about Waldere, and now he has fled and taken dear Hildegund!"

Attila went wild with anger. He ripped off his cloak, rending it to the hem, and his mind shifted this way and that like sand like a sandstorm. His changing face reflecting his feelings – it was white, then red, then white again, sometimes open mouthed and large-eyed in a cry to Tengri; sometimes scrunched up with a furrowed brow, closed eyes and grinding teeth. He was so angry he couldn't speak, and all day long, disdained food and drink. He was so worried, his weary limbs got no rest, and when he retired he couldn't even close his eyes. He tossed and turned in bed, this way and that, like a wounded warrior with a javelin in his breast, then he sat bolt upright. He didn't like that either, so he leapt out of bed, ran about the city, then returned to his bed as restless as ever. The glove side of his nature, the softer side, had been cut to the quick, and he was as upset as a tender-hearted maiden who has been jilted by her lover.

When morning came, however, the other side of his nature, the fist, came to the fore. He called a council of his nobles and said to them: "If anyone will bring Waldere bound like a criminal, I will garb him in gold and send him into my treasury to take his pick!" But there was no-one – no nobleman, soldier or attendant whose eagerness for gain could outweigh his wariness of Waldere, since they had heard that Waldere was armed to the teeth. They had no wish to face him with his sword drawn for they had witnessed his skill in the martial arts both on the parade ground and in Attila's wars.

Attila stared with disbelief at his lords. "What! Is there not one among you who will face Waldere?"

"I will," said a voice from the far end of the table. It was Attila's hostage, Gunther, who had been all but forgotten in the turmoil of the last few days. "I have a score to settle with him."

Gunther had grown up a lot since his army had been defeated and now that he was away from the pernicious influence of Herigend. He was facing up to his responsibilities as a man instead of playing at toy soldiers. He knew that he had little chance of capturing the best of Attila's warriors, but if he failed, he would at least die with honour.

Attila took up the offer with zeal. "If you succeed, Gunther, I will restore you to your kingship and will return all the tribute that I have taken from the Franks since the time of your father, Gebicho. I'll also give you that pearl of Hunnic womanhood, Hildaz."

A great cheer was raised from the others, partly for Attila's generosity, partly for Gunther, but mainly because they were off the hook themselves.

"Then, my lord, with your permission, I will take some of your best men to help me, for as you know, Waldere is no mean warrior, and I will need all the help I can get."

"Take the whole Hunnic army if you will," said Attila. "The thing is to find him and bring him back – alive if you can. I have some interesting tortures in mind!"

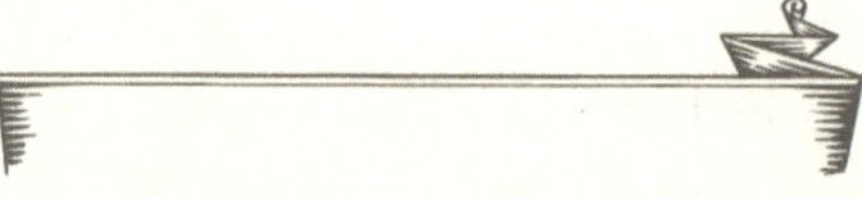

A Garrulous Ferryman

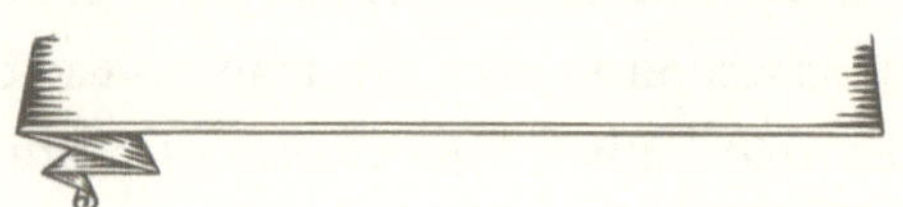

Waldere and Hildegund travelled by night and, by day, hid in the forest. Waldere had worried about Hildegund; about how this fine lady of the court would manage in the wilderness, but she proved to be the scyldmæden they had joked about, and bore the discomfort with a cheerful smile. She caught birds with bird-lime and fish with their fishing rod, while Waldere hunted for game. Then she would cook what they had caught over a small fire, screened with a fence of roughly-plaited branches. She made no complaint about sleeping on the hard, damp ground, saying she had rather sleep there, snuggled up to her lover, than in her downy bed in Attila's palace.

When the sun had finished forty circuits, Waldere and Hildegund at last reached the River Rhine where it wended its way to a city called Worms.

"We will not enter the city," said Waldere, "but cross the river and keep on going to Aquitania."

"But while we are in Burgundia, I would like to see my father," said Hildegund."

"We dare not risk it," said Waldere. "However much he loves you, there is a risk he would return you to Attila. After all, you were well treated there, and he would want to spare his people Attila's reprisals."

Hildegund gave a sad sigh and acknowledged that Waldere was right.

"We will pretend to be common folk and pay the ferryman with fish."

"Then pull that cloak around your armour!"

But it was a poor disguise, for the spears could not be hidden, and the gold rings clinked in the coffers.

At the other side of the river the ferryman said, "That will be three *assi.*"

"Please accept these fish," said Waldere. It was common in those difficult times for people to pay in kind, but the ferryman looked at the fish with surprise. "What sort of fish are these!" he exclaimed. "The Rhine has no such fish! They must be from foreign parts. I'd rather have three of those coins that are clinking in those coffers."

"They are not coins," said Waldere, offering the fish again. "Don't worry, "they are good to eat."

And they were, but the ferryman couldn't get over his disappointment at being paid with three strange fish by a man who was carrying two coffers of what sounded like coins, and he told the story everywhere – and that was how news of Waldere's whereabouts got to Gunther, for the ferryman's description of the traveller was distinctive: a man dressed in warrior's gear with a beautiful woman leading a horse with two coffers strapped to its back that clinked as though they were full of coins.

Gunther set out for Worms at once with his band of retainers. As soon as he got there, he sent for the ferryman and questioned him closely. The ferryman retold his tale, adding, "Something in the coffers clinked like coins. He should have paid me with those and not with his stinking fish!"

"Where did he go next?"

"He followed the road west. It leads to the Vosges."

Gunther thanked him for the information and tossed him a few coins – the cause of more grumbles. As soon as the great man had gone, the Ferryman said, "All I get is a few *assi*.[5] I expected a solidus at least, because there's big money in this, I'll be bound!"

And so the story of the fugitives with the gold coffers, and the man called Gunther who was following them, and who was said to be king of the Franks, continued to circulate, and that's how Hagen heard about it. At first, his loyalties were torn. Should he rejoin his old friend, Waldere, or should he join forces with Gunther, the son of his former king?

He, also, questioned the ferryman to find out which direction to take, and was soon hurrying along the road to the Vosges, leaving a dissatisfied ferryman behind him. "Another few assi! There's money in this! Where's my share? I'm going to go west too and see what I can see!"

By the time Hagen caught up with Gunther he had decided to join him. He had heard how Waldere had made war on his people, though not how he had stopped the defeat turning into a massacre, so he saw him as a friend no longer and wanted to be revenged on him. Hagen found that Gunther was quite different to the foolish youth he had known in Francia. He still had the same boyish looks and scant beard, but there was a dignity about him that he had lacked before: he had grown into a man to be taken seriously and a king to be respected. Gunther was delighted to welcome his old friend, both for himself and for his reputation as a warrior. He now had twelve of Attila's best men to fight on his side, and pressed on with renewed eagerness in pursuit of the fugitives.

Meanwhile, Waldere had got as far as the Vosges, a forested valley, wild and beautiful, where the only sign of human activity were a few simple foresters and the occasional group of hunters, hunting the hart or wild boar. Close by were mountains, and there he saw a cave underneath a rocky outcrop which was protected by a narrow defile that only one man could approach at a time. As soon as he saw it he said: "We'll stay here and hide awhile from pursuers. I'm weary, for since we left the land of the Avars I have had no rest and this war-gear is heavy."

They approached the cave cautiously for it was a likely base for bandits, but they found it empty. They settled down near the entrance to the cave where there was a good view over the valley below. Then Waldere closed his eyes and gratefully lay his head in his loved-one's lap. "Keep careful watch," he warned her. "Wake me if you see anything suspicious." Then he slipped into dreamless sleep.

When Gunther sighted tracks on the ground he urged his horse forward with his spurs, and exulting in spirit, shouted to his retainers, "Quickly, men! Soon we'll catch him!"

Only Hagen had reservations: "I'll tell you one thing, Gunther. If you'd seen him fighting as often as I have, you wouldn't be in such a hurry!"

"I've faced him in battle, and I'll admit he's good, but what can one man do against twelve?"

"You'd be surprised," said Hagen. "He's like a one-man army! I should know. I trained with him!"

Now it had come to the point, he was having doubts about fighting with his old friend. True, he had made war on his kinsmen, but he had been ordered to do it by Attila, and he knew from his own experience that Attila's orders were not lightly contradicted. He tried other arguments, but Gunther refused to take any notice, trusting in his own prowess and the prowess of his warriors. However, it was not the recklessness of youth, or the influence of bad council, it was because Gunther was grimly determined to make up for his youthful folly in breaking the treaty with Attila and bringing war upon his people. He wanted to win back the treasures of the Franks or die with honour.

From their hideaway in the cave, Hildegund saw a cloud of dust on the road, and realized that it must be a group of travellers. She watched it anxiously for a while and soon glints of light showed that it was a band of armed men, the glints being reflections from their helmets and spear points.

She woke Waldere gently and told him what she had seen. He sprang up at once, rubbing the sleep out of his eyes, and reached for his shield, sword and spear. Then, as Attila had taught him, he limbered up, playing with his weapons in preparation for battle, swinging his blade and brandishing his spear. Hildegund watched the weapons whirling so quickly they were just a blur and felt comforted at his skill. After a few minutes of this, Waldere was suddenly still. He took several deep breaths to calm his spirit so that he could enter battle with the focus that Attila taught him.

Hildegund, thinking of her own fate, said, "If they look like winning, kill me! I would rather you severed my neck than be given by another in an arranged marriage – or worse! You know the fate of women who are taken in war!"

Waldere frowned, his mind troubled again. "Shall your innocent blood stain my blade? How can my sword strike down my enemies if it fails to spare a faithful friend! But do not grieve, the All-Father has saved me from worse than this! You'll be safe enough!"

Once again he took deep breaths to calm his spirit, then, scanning ahead to see what his enemies were doing, he saw a familiar crest, and a broad smile lit up his face. "All will be well. Hagen is here." Then his face fell and his mood darkened. "But why? Why is he with my enemies?"

"Because you beat his kinsmen in battle," Hildegund reminded him.

Waldere's face fell and his heart was heavy. Would the twisted warp of wyrd lead him to fight with his best friend? If so, so be it. To protect his woman was his main concern. Turning to her, he said, "Of these war-hardened warriors I fear none but Hagen, for he is as good as me when it comes to the martial arts, and what's worse, he knows my style of fighting. If I can handle him, with God's help, we can get away."

When Hagen saw Waldere looking at him so intently, he pleaded with Gunther: "If you start anything with Waldere, be sure he will finish it! Why don't you send an envoy instead to find out where he is going and what he intends to do? – and also to ask him to hand over the treasure, the gold, and the sword, *Mimming*, in return for free passage. Waldere is a wise man, and I'm sure he'll agree."

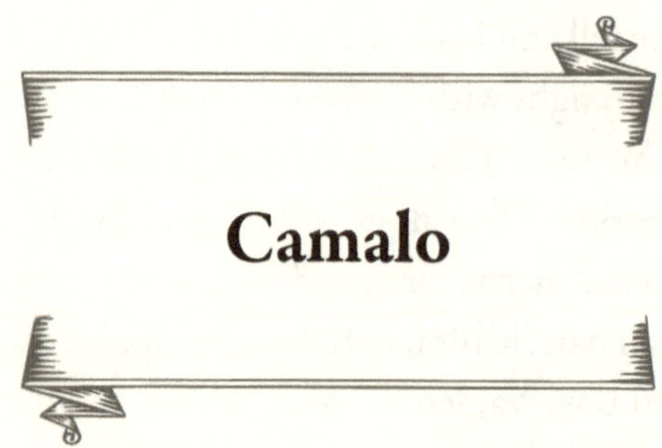

Camalo

Gunther took Hagen's advice and ordered Camalo to go. He was the man who was sent to Mettis as Prefect, arriving when Gunther received the report about the fish. He was a tall man in his middle years, well-muscled and well-armed. Gunther made it quite clear that if Waldere refused the request, he was to kill him on the spot and bring back the gold and the girl.

Camalo mounted his horse and confidently galloped across the field, racing like wind, to where Waldere was waiting. He reined in his horse a few yards in front of Waldere and addressed him as he had been ordered: "Tell me who you are and where are you heading!"

Waldere replied: "I have no idea why you are asking. Cannot travellers pass in peace? However, as it happens, I have nothing to hide. I am Ælfhere's son, from Aquitania, Waldere by name. When I was young I was sent as a hostage to the Huns. I lived with Attila, but now I am on my way home."

Camalo said, "Gunther commands that you give him the sword, *Mimming*, the coffers of gold, and the girl too. If you do this without delay he will spare your life."

Waldere replied like the brave-hearted warrior that he was: "Gunther has promised what he cannot deliver! I am not in a cell or bound in chains, so I can fight back! Well then, listen! If he lets me go without a fight – for I see he is fully armed, and has a band of armed retainers – I'll give him a hundred gold rings."

Camalo smiled to himself as he wheeled his horse. He had not thought that success would be so easy! He rode back and reported to Gunther, confident that he would gladly accept such a generous offer. But Gunther refused even to consider it.

Hagen, still reluctant to make war on his former friend, intervened with well-meant advice: "Take the treasure, Gunther, and let him go. These are kingly gifts which you have won without wasting lives. But don't do anything to awaken Waldere's war-mood or you'll regret it."

Gunther just laughed. "He'll regret it, you mean!"

Hagen tried a different line of persuasion, referring to a dream he had had. It sounded far-fetched, but it was not just rhetoric, it was true; he'd really had that bad dream: "Last night, I dreamed that you fought a fierce bear who bit your leg through to the bone, then attacked me as I came to your aid, biting an eye and breaking my teeth."

Gunther replied with contempt: "Hagen, you're like your father, Hagathie. He too had an over-fearful heart and avoided battles, despite his boasting!"

Hagen grew angry and said, "Very well, then fight! The foe is in sight. Go and get him if you dare! But I will keep out of it!" With those words, he spurred his horse to a nearby hill, where he watched and waited. It was not cowardice, as Gunther had hinted, but a reluctance to fight his former friend, and disgust that Gunther had turned down a generous offer.

Gunther, turning to Camalo, repeated his orders: "Go and tell Waldere to give me all the treasure. Tell him it is mine by right, taken from the Franks by Attila, and taken from Attila by him. If he refuses, kill him!"

So the man of Mettis made his way, well prepared, with his helmet on his head and his war-shirt shining on his chest, but a little less confident than before. He stopped at a safe distance and hailed Waldere in a more conciliatory tone than last time: "Listen, friend, hand over the gold to Gunther. He says it is his by right, so hang on to your life and stay healthy!"

But Waldere did not waste words. He had said all he had to say last time, so he kept silent and waited for his enemy to attack. Camalo rode cautiously forward and repeated his message, and this time Waldere answered him: "What do you want? I've done nothing to harm you, so let me go on my way in peace. Listen! I'll pay for my passage with more gold rings for Gunther: I'll give two hundred, as well as *Mimming*, that magnificent heirloom."

Camalo had his orders and so made a boastful reply: "Either you give everything to King Gunther, or I will spill your blood with this spear."

Attila had taught Waldere that there is a time for words and a time for action, and so he made no reply this time. Camalo waited a moment longer, then threw his spear with all his strength. It was a well-aimed throw, but Waldere stepped adroitly aside, as Attila had trained him, and the spear sank into the soil giving the world a pointless wound.

"If you wish to fight, I'm your man!" cried Waldere, and hurled his spear with such strength and accuracy that it went right through Camalo's shield. Camalo had just begun to draw his sword, and now his hand was pinned by the point of the spear through hand and leg and into his horse. The horse reared up and whinnied in pain, shaking the rider, but the spear shaft held him. Camalo then cast aside his shield, and with his left hand, heaved at the spear to pull it out. Waldere, taking the opportunity, grabbed Camalo's foot, and thrust his sword into the man's breast. As he drew out his weapon, he removed his spear, and both foe and horse fell to the ground. The horse was wounded, but Camalo lay dead.

Kimo

When Camalo's nephew, a man called Kimo, saw this, he groaned, and with a grim expression on his face, called: "Camalo meant more to me than any other man alive. So now I shall die or avenge my kinsman!"

He was a young warrior, with a fresh, beardless face, but the scars on his arms showed that he was no stranger to battle. Like Camalo, he went alone, for no-one could aid another man in the narrow defile near the cave. He rode towards Waldere brandishing two spears with wide blades, but when he saw him unworried by fear, standing firm in the same place, he gnashed his teeth and nodded his head, shaking the horsehair crest of his helm, and said, "In what gods do you trust that you dare defy me? I don't want your gold or your goods, I want only my just revenge!"

In truth he was unnerved by Waldere's bold stance. Kimo had practiced handling two spears at the same time, while controlling his horse with his knees. Just the sight of him with spears held high in both hands was enough to make his enemies quail, but Waldere (who could do the same) seemed unmoved. He merely replied in a conciliatory voice: "If I had started this fight, I would indeed deserve to die, but Gunther gave the word, and your kinsman started it!" He had not finished speaking when Kimo flung both of his spears at him. But Waldere dodged one and deflected the other with his own spear held in the high guard that Attila had taught him.

Kimo, seeing the skill with which Waldere did this, would have turned away, but he was aware of Gunther's eyes upon him and felt that he had no choice but to press the attack. So he unsheathed his sword and galloped towards Waldere, whirling his sword in a typical Hunnic attack. But Waldere held him off with his spear which had a longer reach. Kimo tried to knock it aside with his sword, but Waldere parried the blow and used his left hand to thrust the butt of the spear at Kimo's leg. The blow also hit the horse's belly, and it reared dangerously, its hooves whirling. Waldere backed off, but not quickly enough to escape the whirling hooves, which knocked his spear out of his hand. It was a dangerous moment. Kimo saw his advantage, and swung his sword with all his might, intending to split Waldere's skull, but the blow was ill-aimed and lacked force, and slid off harmlessly off Waldere's helmet. Quickly, Waldere picked up his spear and went onto the attack. Kimo tried to turn his horse, but he was hampered by the narrow defile and dropped his guard as he struggled with the reins. It was only for the briefest moment, but Waldere, quick as lightening, thrust with his spear and caught him under his chin, half-severing his head and knocking him off his horse. He was done for, anyway, but Waldere made assurance sure by hacking off his head. Kimo's last sight was his own fresh blood mixed with the dried blood of his kinsman, Camalo.

Werinhard

When Gunther saw this, he encouraged his wavering warriors to renew the fight: "Let's keep attacking him until he grows tired. Then we can finish him off." So a third man went, whose name was Werinhard, son of Pandares, another arrogant youth, boastful but with little experience of battle. Nevertheless, he was well-armed and well-trained, and not to be underestimated.

This man spurned to fight with a spear, and went into battle Hunnic style, on horseback with a bow and quiver, fighting from afar in the way that Nordic warriors consider cowardly. But Waldere took shelter behind his large Frankish shield and with great skill fended off the arrows, dodging them, or deflecting them. When Werinhard's quiver was empty, he unsheathed his sword and shouted, "You fended off my arrows, Waldere, but are you able to block my blows?"

"A fair fight," said Waldere calmly, "Is what I've been waiting for! Wield your weapon!" When he had spoken, he flung his spear which buried itself in the horse's breast. The steed rose up, unseated its rider, whipped the air with whirling hooves, then fell on top of him. Waldere strode towards him, snatched away his sword, knocked off his helm, and grabbed his hair, and the son of Pandares, so lately boasting, was now pleading for his life.

"Very well," said Waldere. "I said I was waiting for a fair fight. Now get up, take your sword and let us fight man to man."

He gave Werinhard a few minutes to collect himself and arrange his war-gear, then sprang to the attack. He used the fast, swirling strokes that Attila had taught him, and soon found that Werinhard, however good with a bow, was no swordsman. He flailed without purpose, his strokes landed harmlessly on Waldere's shield, or were blocked by his well-judged guards. Werinhard was less sure with his guards and took a number of serious thrusts to his breast which would have finished him had it not been for his lamellar armour. Nevertheless, he felt the force of the blows, and staggered backwards, struggling to keep his balance and maintain his guard.

"Give up!" cried Waldere. "You are beaten and you know it! Put up your sword and swear not to fight me again, and I will spare you."

"Never!" gasped Werinhard, though he knew that his only hope was to strike a lucky blow. He lunged wildly, but Waldere turned the thrust aside with the rim of his shield and made a well-aimed cut across Werinhard's throat. It severed the vein and blood gushed out in a fountain as Werinhard fell to the ground. Waldere could not risk his enemy recovering and attacking him again, so he finished him off by severing his head.

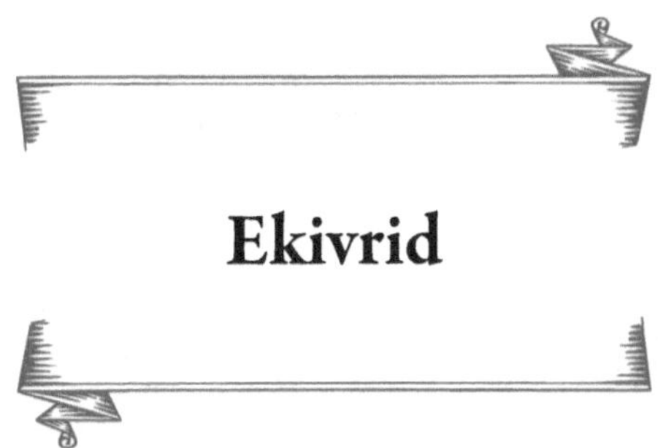

Ekivrid

Three down! But that did not bother Gunther, who still had some of his old recklessness. He sent another man, Ekivrid, to face his fate, promising him Waldere's arms and armour as trophies. Ekivrid was a Saxon who had killed a man and been sent into exile. He was a fearsome sight, heavy as a ox, covered in scars, and with a face set in a permanent scowl above his grizzled beard. He had never taken to Hunnic arms and armour, and wore a Saxon byrnie, carried a huge bullhide-covered shield and hefted a heavy broadsword.

When he saw Waldere splattered with Werinhard's blood, he said, "Are you human, an evil elf, or one of those outlaws who haunt the forest that you slay men so easily?"

Waldere laughed as he replied, "Your Saxon war-gear suggest that you might be a worthy warrior, but if you come too close and my hand touches you, you will leave the Vosges to fly to Valhalla!"

"I'll soon find out," said the Saxon, as he cast his iron-tipped cornel-wood out of the thong of his throwing strap. But Waldere caught it on the iron boss of his shield, and the spearhead shattered, once again, his training in dodging and deflecting weapons paying off. Then, in the blink of an eye, he had sent a spear of his own. Its blade split Ekivrid's bullhide-covered shield, but was stopped by his well-forged byrnie.

Ekrivid then drew his sword and boasted, "This sword of mine, *Skull-Scraper*, will shatter that puny Hunnic thing – and then your skull!"

Waldere knew that his shield must bear the brunt of the attack, as his urepos was ill suited to block such a heavy blade. Ekrivid proved to be an accomplished swordsman, Saxon style: slow, but steady and strong, every blow taking a heavy toll. More than once he got through Waldere's guard, and only his Weland-wrought war-shirt, Ælfhere's heirloom, saved his life. Waldere played a defensive game for a while, letting Ekrivid use up his strength, then, when he judged the moment right, he went onto the attack, Hunnic style, as Attila had taught him, whirling his urepos in an invisible blur and dancing around his opponent. He had the advantage that Ekrivid's shield was split, and all he had left was the iron boss, but though he scored many hits, his light urepos couldn't penetrate that hard and hand-riveted byrnie. Ekrivid even laughed at his attempts, fending off his thrusts with shield boss or blade, and waiting for an opening. It came when he pushed Waldere's blade wide with his shield boss so that it was horizontally in front of him. In an instant he smashed his heavy broadsword onto the *urepos*, knocking it out of Waldere's hand. Waldere, backed off immediately, and looked round for help. Luckiily, Hildegund had been watching, and had a spear ready. He took the spear and was just in time to wield it against Ekrivid as he charged, sword held high, for the killer blow. The combined force of Ekrivid's onrush and Waldere's thrust was enough to pierce Ekrivid's ring-mail and his breast. He rolled over and retched blood, tugging frantically at the spear, but his hands went limp, and his chin slumped on his chest. It had been a close thing, but the bear-like Saxon was dead.

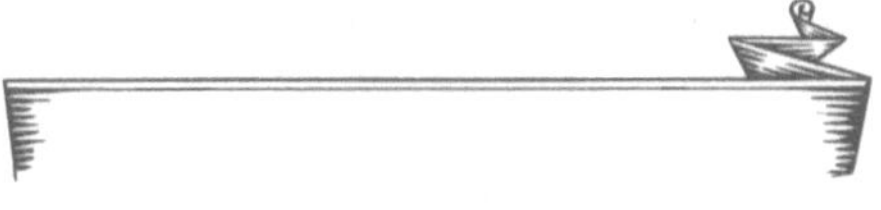

Hadawart

Waldere was badly bruised after that close-fought bout and drained of energy, but Attila had taught him to bear hardship, and so he looked to his defences. He drove his enemy's horse away, and retrieved his spear, only to find a fifth enemy approaching. His name was Hadawart. He was a hardened warrior; a veteran of many battles, but when he saw the bodies blocking his horse's way, his heart missed a beat. Nevertheless, he steeled himself, dismounted and proceeded on foot.

Waldere awaited him, praising his foe for fighting fairly, instead of charging on a horse. Hadawart replied, hoping to avoid combat with this master of marshal arts: "Hear my proposal: put down your shield, give us the gold and go free. I don't want to hurt so heroic a man, Attila's famed *ordwyga*, but I am a hero too, with many victories to my credit. See these arm-rings, all of gold. Each one is a victory-gift. But if it happens that you take my life, my comrades will never let you leave in one piece!"

Waldere replied, not directly, but with an invocation to his own prowess: "O right hand, rain blows on my enemy so that he may not take the towers of my wall! O left hand, grip the shield as though glued to the handle! Do not lose the load you have lifted so long over so many paths from the place of the Avars!"

"If you refuse, Waldere," continued Hadawart, "You will lose your war-gear and your horse to me; and everything else – all your goods, the girl and the gold – to Gunther."

Then he stripped his sword from its sheath and they flashed together like lightening bolts in a thunderstorm. They were great in spirit and grand in arms; the one with a sword, the other with a spear. They strove mightily, striking each other with fearful strength: like the sound of the holm-oak hacked by the axe was the sound of hammering on helmets and shields. The Huns watched in wonderment, amazed that Waldere was not worn out, though he'd already battled with four war-hardened warriors.

In truth, Waldere was worn out, and though he fought on, he was less strong in attack, less quick in recovering his guard, and less agile in manouvring around his enemy; so it was not long before Hadawart, saw an opening in Waldere's defence. He wielded his sword for the killer blow, but Waldere managed to blocked it with his spear at high guard, and the shock of it, running along the blade into the hilt, caused Hadawart to drop his sword, which bounced away into the bushes. Hadawart hurried after it, but Waldere, calling on his last reserves of strength, sped after him calling: "Don't shy away, come and get my war-gear!" As he spoke, he lunged with his spear, and Hadawart fell with his shield on top of him. Waldere, too tired to show mercy, stepped on his neck, pulled away the shield, and shoved his spear right through his body. The man rolled back, breathed his last, and his spirit left him.

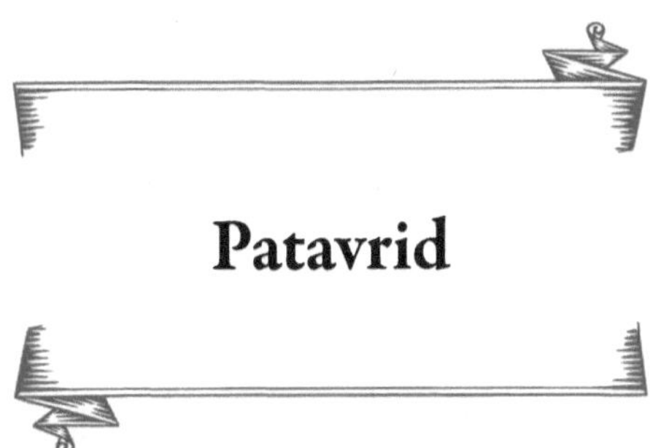

Patavrid

The sixth was Patavrid, Hagen's nephew and his sister's protégée. When he saw him preparing for battle, Hagen begged him to stop. "What are you doing? See how Death grins! Can't you see wyrd weaving your last thread? Dear nephew, your mind deceives you if you think you are a match for a man like Waldere!"

But Patavrid spurned this advice because he was young and foolish and greedy for glory – though perhaps, Hagen reflected, that is a nobler motive than being greedy for gold, as Gunther was. Greed for gold! – the heart of all evil! You inflame men to such an extent that they do not fear to meet death in their greed for gain, and the more they drink of it, the more they die of thirst! They take by force, and sometimes by fraud, causing more tears, and toil and trouble than any natural disaster. The lust for glory is just as bad, and there is an example: I cannot call back my beloved nephew for he is burning with it! He will risk everything for a panegyric in a saga! Alas, Patavrid, what of your mother; what of your newly wedded wife who has, as yet, no child to cheer her? What is this madness? – what makes you do it?

These were Hagen's bitter thoughts as he watched his nephew ride to certain death. "Goodbye, my boy, may the All-Father go with you," he called after him, sobbing aloud and not caring if it seemed unmanly.

Though far away, Waldere saw his friend trying to talk his nephew into seeing sense, and he dearly hoped he would succeed, both for Patavrid's sake, and for his own – for the five combats had left him feeling as tired as Rip Van Winkle before he slept for a hundred years.

But he saw Hagen's gestures of despair, and the young man turn away and mount his horse. Even then he hoped he could persuade him to see sense, so he hailed him as he approached: "Stop! Save yourself for something better! You are deceived! Look at these dead! Go back or you will lie with them!"

But Patavrid took no notice. He had that youthful arrogance that believes it will carry all before it. He knew Waldere's reputation as a warrior, but that was all in the past. It was time for these older men to acknowledge their weakness and make way for shining youth. With these thoughts in mind, he ignored Waldere's warning and threw his spear with all his might.

But he had misjudged the range. Twelve paces is the maximum for an accurate throw, and he was at least 20 paces away. So the spear lost momentum and Ælfhere's son knocked it aside as easily as if he was training with Attila. It flew away in an arcing dance, hitting the ground near Hildegund's feet. She cried out in fear, but finding her scyldmæden spirit, pulled the spear out of the ground and held it out, ready to protect herself.

Patravrid used his sword for his next attack, swinging it high in the hope of a cut to Waldere's head. But Waldere swung his war-board to catch the blow, rather than waste what little energy he had left in the the thrust and parry of swordplay. Patravrid, eager for glory, tried again, raining dozens of blows on Waldere, but Waldere continued to shelter under his shield, fending off the youth's fine steel, waiting for him to tire or to make a mistake. The foolish youth thought he had the advantage. Here he was, hammering his enemy, while his enemy seemed unable to fight back. But the moment came when he lost his guard and left an opening. In an instant Waldere attacked with a mighty swing that halved Patavrid's shield. Now Patavrid was at a disadvantage as the unbalanced board was little use as a defence, and it was Waldere's turn to go onto the attack. But before he did, he backed off, and tried to persuade him to lay down his arms.

"You are my old friend's nephew, and I don't want to hurt you. You fought well. Leave it at that. I will not even ask you to surrender. Just go back to Hagen and stay there."

"Never!" screamed Patavrid.

"That's just what Werinhard said," sighed Waldere, "and look – there is his head!"

Were those tears rolling down Patavrid's cheeks as he sprang into a frenzied attack? Perhaps, but soon to be tears of blood. Waldere heaved a great sigh. Its ounded like despair to Patavrid, but it was pity. Even now, he tried to spare him, even though it was at his own expense, wasting what little energy he had left. He struck again and again at Patavrid's shield, trying to wear him down in the hope that he'd give up. He could have slashed his throat, as he had done with Werinhard, but wanted to defeat this foolish youth rather than kill him. But the Hunnic lamellar cuirass is nowhere near as strong as a ring-mail byrnie, and a horizontal cut, that Patavrid failed to catch on his shield, sliced through the gap between the platelets, laying bare his belly.

Unlucky Patavrid, seeing his own guts spilling out, collapsed to the ground, giving his body to the sylvan beasts – as for his soul, who can say where it went and on what strange journey?

Waldere was troubled. He hated to see this fine young man dead in the dust as a result of his own handiwork, but he had done his best to spare him – and had paid for it. Now his muscles were trembling with weariness, and he felt as though a little child could have pushed him over. He wanted nothing more than to throw himself down and sleep!

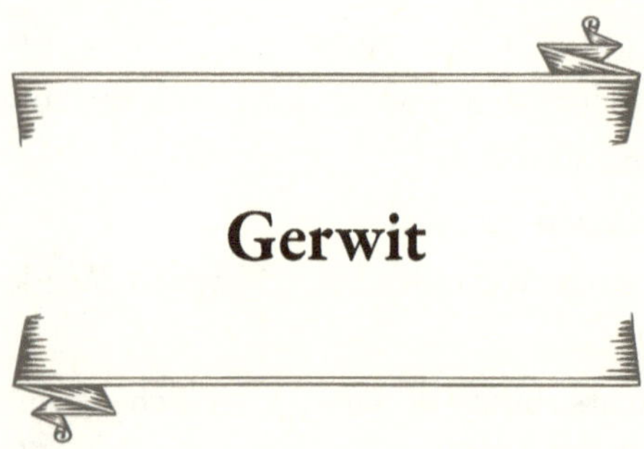

Gerwit

B ut it was not to be, for Gerwit, a much-feared warrior, rode forward toget revenge for Patavrid. He was the Count of Worms, a stern man in his middle years, who had led many armies into battle and never lost a fight. He was another Germanic warrior, his preferred weapon being a double-headed axe – a fearsome weapon! Just one look at it was enough to make an untried warrior cry for his mother. As for Waldere, the very sight of that weapon of destruction sent a flood of nervous energy through his veins. He was still weary unto death, but knew that he must somehow find the strength to hold out. He decided that his best tactic was to go on the defensive and let his best ally, his shield, bear the brunt of the attack.

Gerwit's strong horse, a large courser, quite different from the small Hunnic horse, leapt over the bodies which had blocked the narrow bridleway, and cantered towards Waldere. Waldere knew that he must keep out of the reach of that terrible double-axe at all costs, so he flung his spear before Gerwit could get to him. However, Gerwit was a seasoned warrior and managed to dodge it. Then he galloped at Waldere whirling his axe. The fight was fearful! It was two-handed axe against sword and shield. There were no words this time; they hadn't the breath. Gerwit struck to avenge his comrades, and Waldereheld up his shield to shelter his body, and if wyrd willed, to win the victory: one strikes a blow, the other blocks; one thrusts, the other leans away. Cunning and courage are equal on both sides and the outcome is uncertain. Waldere manages to fend of the axe with the iron boss of his wooden shield, while he looks for a chance to use his sword. Gerwit, also hoping to trick his opponent, circles on, swirling his battle-axe.

It was an unequal contest: Gerwit on a horse with a double-headed axe, and Waldere on foot with sword and shield; Gerwit fresh to the fight, and Waldere half dead with weariness. No wonder that Waldere felt that he was getting the worse of it, and this hand-to-hand combat was likely to finish him off. So he backed off and reached for his second spear, which Hildegund held ready for him. This time, he used the spear as a thrusting weapon, wielded in both hands, leaving his shield behind. He had only his dancing moves now to escape the whirling axe, as Gerwit tried, sometimes to chop his spear in half, and sometimes to chop his head in half – but he knew he would not be able to keep it for long.

Gerwit had a small round shield slung over his shoulder, but he couldn't use it and wield his heavy axe at the same time. And though his horse gave him the advantage of height, it limited his manouvreabily, so it was not long before Waldere gained the advantage. He could stay out of reach of that terrible axe, and prod his enemy at will, all the time being careful that Gerwit didn't chop his spear in half.

Gerwit, frustrated at his inability to get close enough to strike the killer blow, whipped his horse and made a sudden charge. Waldere responded by thrusting at his thigh. Gerwit fell backward with a gut-wrenching cry, and tumbled to the ground, wounded, but still very much alive. But before he could get up, Waldere drew his sword and hacked off his head, leaving for worms the Count of Worms. Then he went back to the cave, hoping at last to rest his worn and weary limbs.

When the others saw the fate of Gerwit, they began to falter and begged their lord to depart from battle. Gunther flew into a fury: "If I leave the Vosges, where shall I go? It would be inglorious to give in now! I would rather die than depart with dishonour! Why should

Waldere get away without paying the price? Up until now you were burning for his treasure. Burn again men! Burn to honour the blood that was spilled in the spoils of death! Let your blows console your murdered comrades!"

Just then, the ferryman caught up with them, and recognizing Gunther, said, "My lord, I have been looking for you."

"Well, what is it?" said Gunther, whose mind was on the battle with Waldere.

The ferryman spoke in wheedling words, accompanied by an obsequious bow. "You gave me a few assi, but I have heard that there is money in this, big money. Will you not give me a solidus?"

Gunther laughed. "You are right about the money – a fortune in gold rings – but it is that man over there who has them. Go and ask him for one."

The ferryman set off in the direction that Gunther had indicated, but he had not gone far before he came to the body of Camalo, and a little further on the headless body of Kimo.

"What's this!" he said aloud. "It's a high price to pay for a gold ring! I'll leave these nobles to their butcher's work and get back to ferrying!" And with those words he ran away, and never again interfered in the business of his passengers.

Randolf

While this was happening the exhausted hero put down his weapons, removed his helm and hung it on a tree, caught his breath and wiped his brow. He asked Hildegund to bring wine and to keep a sharp lookout.

"Surely Gunther will give up now that seven of his men lay dead!" she said.

"I hope so," said Waldere, "I can hardly move for weariness!" and with these words he leaned back against a rock and closed his eyes.

But he rested too soon, for Randolf, who was renowned as an athlete, saw that Waldere was off guard and thought to use his speed to take him by surprise. Spear in hand, he crept as close as he could under cover, moving from bush to bush, then, when there was no more cover, sprinted as fast as he could towards Waldere.

"Watch out!" screamed the ever-vigilant Hildegund.

Waldere had not rested long, but it had been enough to give him back his energy. He was on his feet in a moment, but Randolf was now in range, and threw his spear with all his might. It struck Waldere in the chest, and if Ælfhere's heirloom war-net had not protected him, the spear would have pierced his breast. Still reeling from the blow, he grabbed his shield and drew his sword, though he hadn't had time to put on his helmet, for Randolf was upon him, his sword swinging wildly.

Waldere held his best friend, his shield, high and caught Randolf's wild blows, while looked for an opening to strike back. Randolf thought to take advantage of the fact that Waldere's head was unprotected, and made a series of left and right cuts over the top of his shield. Waldere ducked, but one of Randolf's strokes scraped Waldere's head and sliced off a lock of his hair, but did no more harm. Randolf struck again, but Waldere smashed his wrist with his iron shield boss causing Randolf to drop his sword. Waldere now moved in close and tripped Randolf up with a kick to his left calf, causing him to fall on his back. He lay there spread-eagled and pleading for mercy, but Waldere felt no sympathy for this man who had tried to trick him, so he stepped on his chest and said, "Thanks for the haircut, now I'll cut yours!" and he severed Randolf's head, paying no heed to his blubbered pleas.

Helmnod, Trogus and Tanastus

Helmnod came next – the ninth attacker Waldere had faced that day, and it was clear that he intended to try something different. He was wielding a trident tied to a rope, which was held by others standing behind him; his plan was to pull Waldere's shield away, leaving him vulnerable to attack. He threw the trident, calling out boldly, "Listen to me, baldy! Under this iron you will find your end!" The trident flashed like a javelin, slammed into the wood of the shield – and stayed there, the barbs on its three prongs holding it tightly. The Huns shouted with joy, heaving together to part Waldere from his best ally. Even Gunther took part. Rivers of sweat seeped down their limbs, but still the hero stood his ground, like a well-rooted tree against roaring winds. His eager enemies encouraged each other to pull away his shield, or drag him to his death in the open field. But the son of Ælfhere was boiling with anger and, though his head was bare of its helmet and he had no spear, only a sword, he suddenly let go of his shield and the three men staggered backwards.

Waldere took advantage of their disarray to attack the foremost, which was Helmnod. He raised his sword high and with the combined force of his running attack and his downward swing, he split Helmnod's skull, cut through his chin, his neck and his chest. Helmnod slumped to the ground, his heart stopped beating and he gave up his breath. Waldere was as surprised as the others. He had not thought that the urepos, the light Hunnic sword, was capable of such a deep cut.

But there was no time for reflection. He still had the advantage of surprise and he intended to make the most of it. Trogus, who in the tug of war had foolishly taken off his sword so that it wouldn't get in the way, was hurrying to recover it, but Waldere excelled in speed as he did in swordplay, and he didn't spare himself. When Trogus was just about in reach, Waldere attempted a slashing blow and managed to slice his calves, slowing him down. Then he stole his shield and was glad to have a new ally. Trogus, though weakened by the wound, was determined to fight back, and seeing a huge stone, he snatched it up and flung it at Waldere, splitting his own shield into splinters, though the bull's hide cover held the wood together. It was enough for Waldere, who strode forward to finish the job. This was too much for Trogus, and he gave up the fight, shouting with terror, "Here, take my sword! Though mark you, it is Fate that has undone me, not you!"

Waldere ignored him. He was not in the mood to show mercy to these men who had tried to disarm him with their trident, and attack him three against one, rather than fight fairly. He raised his sword and was just about to strike the killer blow, when somebody shoved another shield in the way – the third man, Tanastus, had joined the fray.

Waldere turned his sword on him, and finding Tanastus' left side exposed because of the way he had stretched out to protect Trogus, sliced through his side and spilled his guts. "Farewell," he whispered as Tanastus toppled forward to lie writhing in agony on the ground. "Now, where was I?" he said to himself, and turned back to Trogus, who bellowed bitter abuse, knowing that he would be next.

Waldere simply said: "Die! and take this message with you to the All-Father. Waldere sends his greetings and thanks you for your protection." Then he struck the killer blow, and the two men lay dead in the dust with their heels twitching.

Seeing this, Gunther's grim resolve began to falter. He remembered vividly how Waldere had defeated him in Francia, and saw the same horror playing out before his eyes. In Francia his whole army had been destroyed, and now it was his whole war troop, of which only Hagen was left. It is easy to say "death or dishonor" when you have a chance of victory, but when defeat is certain the prospect of death does not look so attractive. He would have to give up his dream of returning to Francia as king with all the treasures of the Franks, but he had escaped Attila, and had enough to live anonymously in some remote region.

But Hagen would have none of it and begged him to continue the battle, for after the death of his nephew, Patavrid, that fair and innocent youth, his anger at Waldere was reawakened, and he felt an overpowering urge to seek revenge. "If you leave now, the many foes that used to fear the Huns will say that our war-band was wiped out by the hand of one man – think of that, Gunther!"

Hagen was not unaware of the irony that, not so long ago, he had tried to persuade Gunther to leave Waldere in peace, and now he was trying to persuade him to fight on – but it made little difference because Gunther could not be convinced: "Who was ever so foolish as to jump in a fire of his own free will? For fighting Waldere would be just like that! He is sure to win! He has shown us that!"

"Perhaps we can beat him if we try something different," said Hagen. "Let's ride away, and after a while, when Waldere thinks we've gone for good, he will come out of his stronghold – and when he comes out, we can take him by surprise. He will never beat two of us if we can catch him on open ground!"

Gunther pondered this plan for a long while before the hope of regaining his honour and his kingship stirred again, and at last he agreed to it.

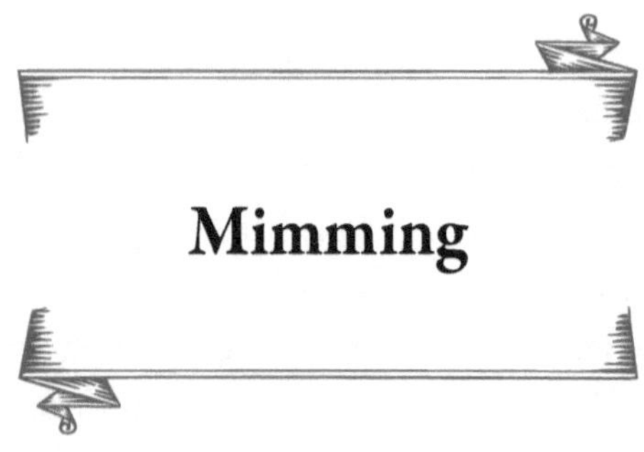

Mimming

When the world-gem had sunk to the western shore and a shining star showed the way, Waldere wondered whether it would be a good time to risk travelling on, or whether it would be better to stay in his stronghold. His mind was like a stormy sea tossed with waves of worry, weighing every risk, but fearing only Hagen. He was still unsure of his enemy's intentions. Had Gunther gone for good, or would he come back with more men, or perhaps plan an ambush? Another problem was that the forest was unfamiliar, with dangerous places and difficult paths, the threat of thorn-bushes and wild beasts.

After considering these things for a long time, he came to a decision and told it to Hildegund: "However it turns out with Hagen and Gunther, I shall take some rest until day returns and then we will try to travel home. Then, at least, Gunther won't be able to say I fled like a thief in the night."

Waldere renewed his barricade with freshly cut thorns woven together, and when he had finished that, he went to the dead warriors, and, sighing with sorrow, particularly for the young and innocent Patavrid, put their heads, which were lying around like so many scattered rocks, back with the bodies they belonged to, and with his sword held upright in his hand said a prayer to the All-Father: "I thank you for protecting me against their unjust blows, but do not destroy them for their ill-advised deeds. Pardon their sins and grant them peace in the Hereafter."

After saying this prayer he took the horses of his attackers and tied them with twigs. Only six remained, for two had been slain, and Gunther had driven three away. This done, he loosened his belt and relaxed his body, and with reassuring words to Hildegund, took some food and fell asleep, having asked her to take the first watch. He intended to wake for the morning watch, which is the most dangerous time of day. Then he fell asleep, Hildegund watching at his head, singing softly to keep herself awake.

An hour before dawn, Waldere got up to keep his watch. Sometimes he went where the horses were tethered, sometimes he listened intently, leaning on the barrier, longing for the world-candle to rise above the horizon so that any threats would be easy to see.

At last the sun rose, and as all seemed quiet, Waldere decided that it was safe to leave the defile, and so he packed his few possessions and set off as before, with himself in full armour, and Hildegund leading *Lion*, and carrying the fishing rod. As they walked, Hildegund kept looking anxiously behind her. "I'm sure we are being followed," she said.

Waldere scanned the valley and seeing nothing, reassured her. "I can't see anything. Come on, Hildegund, where's that scyldmæden spirit?"

That little jest reassured her for a while, but she still had an uneasy feeling, and still kept looking round. Then she saw them: two armed men coming up the hill at a hurried pace. White-faced with fear she cried: "Two men! We've had it if we can't get away!"

Waldere turned, and sure enough, there were was Gunther and Hagen. He breathed a sigh that was almost despairing and said, "All that fighting was for nothing if we should die in the end. But how can I fight them? I have only one spear left and my urepos is all but done for: it was never designed for such heavy work. It is badly notched and as blunt as a fish knife."

Hildegund urged him to fight on, inspired with a new idea: "Take the sword, *Mimming* and don't spare it! Use it savagely to save our lives! Surely, Weland's work will never weaken. That sword is a hard-edged sword and is famous for the heroes it has cut down!"

Waldere was heartened to hear these words and went to get the sword, while Hildegund continued to urge him. "Attila's best warrior, show your bravery! Do not despair! The day has come when your wyrd will lead you, either to loss of life, or lasting glory among the men of Middle Earth. Never let it be said that I saw you shrink from swordplay, however many men attack you! Think of honour, of glory, and God will help you! – and you won't have to worry about your sword: *Mimming* was sent to help us! Use it on Gunther! He sought this fight! I can't believe that he refused the sword and 200 rings of gold!"

"He had his mind on greater treasures!" said Waldere with a wry grimace. "Think of the rewards Attila would shower on him if he brought us back in chains!"

Hildegund gave a bitter laugh, "Gunther is more likely to leave here ringless – what will he tell Attila then?"

But Waldere had turned his attention to Gunther, who was striding towards them with his sword drawn. He took *Mimming* from Hildegund, drew it from its sheath, and for a moment, admired the beautiful gold-wound hilt, and the twisting grey dragons on its ancient blade – a sign of pattern welding, in which bars of metal are braided like a girl's hair, then hammered into shape, making a sword that is strong, springy and flexible, yet with a hard edge.

Seeing this, Gunther said, "I see you stole *Mimming*. It's a famous blade, but so is mine! *Bloodsnake*! No better sword was ever made. Theodoric thought to send it to Widia himself as a gift fit for a king! *Mimming* will be no match for it, and you will be no match for me! I'll drag you in chains to Attila and claim your arms and armour as a trophy to hang in my hall!"

Waldere said, with the calmness that Attila had taught him: "My war-shirt is Ælfhere's heirloom – take it if you dare!" Then he said to Hildegund: "Take *Lion's* reins and run to safety to the nearby wood while I welcome these fools with Weland's work – no words are sharper!"

Gunther replied in his haughtiest manner: "What are you going to do now, fugitive? Your den is far away! Now you must fight in the open!"

Waldere defied him by ignoring him and addressing Hagen. "I have words for you, Hagen. Wait awhile! Why is my faithful friend now my foe? To think that I said to myself many times: 'I fear no harm while Hagen lives!' I beg you now by our boyhood training, come to your senses! If you agree, I'll reward you with the rings which Gunther refused, and you'll leave this place rich in gold and richer in honour!"

Hagen replied with a grim look, "I had almost forgiven you for making war on my kinsmen – I know what Attila is like! So when Gunther's men attacked you, I rode away – but when you killed that promising youth, my nephew, Patavrid, you destroyed our pact of friendship. Now I seek vengeance! Now deeds shall speak!"

With that, he readied himself for battle, as did Gunther. Waldere too prepared his war-gear. All three of them waiting anxiously, for despite their bold speeches, they knew all too well each other's prowess.

Gunther gave a signal to Hagen and they attacked together, rushing at Waldere, one on each side to hinder his sword strokes. He was like a bear surrounded by hounds in the hunt; they fear his claws but dare not close. Nor did Waldere wish to close with his attackers; they worked well as a team and it was all he could do to hold them off.

The conflict went on in this way for a long time, wearing them down with the toil of battle, the burning sun, the threat of danger, and the fear of death, until the ninth hour, when Waldere said to himself: "If it carries on like this they'll tire me out, so I must force the issue!" Then he leapt forward in a sudden attack and shattered Gunther's shield with his famous sword. The next stroke, aimed low, cut off his leg leaving only a stump of thigh, which gushed so much blood it turned the grass red. Gunther fell at Waldere's feet, where he rolled and screamed in unspeakable agony. Hagen, was horrified to see it, but he had no time to help his companion because Waldere was coming for him, *Mimming* raised for a mighty blow. There was no time to parry the stroke. All that Hagen could do was to bend his head forward and take the blow on his helmet. Luckily, it was an ancient heirloom, finely forged, with many dents that showed how it had protected the warriors of old, and it saved his life. *Mimming* flew apart in a shower of shards which sparkled in the air, but one of the splinters gouged out an eye, and the jagged remnant sliced his lips and knocked out six teeth.

When the hero saw this jagged remnant, he groaned with despair, and despite its wound gold hilt, cast it aside. But when the hero extended his hand, Hagen saw his chance and hacked it off: and so the strong hand of Waldere fell in the dust; a hand that was hated by tyrants; a hand that had held numerous trophies; a hand that had hacked off the heads of his late attackers – but Waldere ignored the pain, as Attila had taught him from those days of the morning bath in the mountain stream, and stuck the bloody stump into his shield-strap, holding his akinakes in his unharmed left hand.

Blood was streaming from Hagen's eye socket so that he could hardly see. "Pax!" he spluttered through his bloody mouth, backing off. Had it been any other man, Waldere would have finished him there and then, as he had done with his other attackers. But his heart went out to his friend, so he sheathed his akinakes, and that was the end of it. Each of the three men was marked with battle. There lay Waldere's hand, there lay Hagen's eye, and there lay Gunther's leg. All three were in agony, but at a word from Waldere, Hildegund ran to help them. She went to Gunther first, who was losing blood so quickly that he was close to fainting. She tied a tourniquet round his stump and bandaged the end with strip of material torn from her kirtle. Fortunately, it was a clean blow, thanks to the sharpness of *Mimming*, and there was every chance that it would heal quickly. Hagen was next. She placed a pad over his empty eye socket and a bandage over that. Finally, she tied a tourniquet round Waldere's wrist, fighting back tears when she saw how her hero had suffered.

When she had finished Waldere asked for a drink: "Fetch some wine, and offer it to my friend Hagen first, and then to Gunther, who after all, was only trying to recover what Attila had taken from him!"

Gunther, though still in great pain, managed a grim smile and said, "Waldere should be first. He must be exhausted after the way we harried him!"

"While we are arguing we could have drained a wine butt!" said Waldere, with wry humour. Hagen took up the jesting tone: "Henceforth you will hunt many a hart," he said, "and make many gloves with their hides. You can stuff your right glove to give the appearance of a hand and hold Hildegund with the other."

Waldere laughed: "As for you, you'll see everything with a sideways glance! – but at least you have one eye left!"

"And I still have one leg," said Gunther through gritted teeth, "and I know a man who can make me another – then watch out if I kick you!" When he had said this, he winced with pain and closed his eyes.

"We must put him on his horse," said Waldere. "Help me, Hagen, for I have only one hand."

"You will have to see for me," replied Hagen because everything looks lopsided.

"Where will we take him?" said Hildegund.

"First to Worms to get him a surgeon, and when he has recovered enough to travel, he can go back to Pannonia."

Gunther opened his eyes. "I can't go there!" he said in a panic. "Do you think Attila will welcome me? Listen, there is something you should know: I did not come after you as Attila's agent, or for greed of gold, but to restore my honour and reclaim the treasure of the Franks."

"Than you have achieved your aims," said Waldere. "You have restored your honour, and I will share the treasure equally with the three of you."

"But I cannot return as king," said Gunther, "because Attila will make war on the Franks again."

"Then join me," said Waldere. "I plan to return to Aquitania, raise an army and join the alliance that Aetius is building against Attila. I'm sure that my kinsman, Theodoric will also give his support, for he fears Attila more than the Romans."

"I will. Then one day, perhaps..." He was going to repeated his dream of returning to Francia as king, but he passed out.

"What about you, Hagen?" said Waldere.

"Francia is a client state again," he said bitterly. "There's nothing I can do there. I will follow my king into exile."

All three of them had grievous wounds, but the wounds of grievance were healed by that brief conversation, and they became firm friends and allies.

As soon as they were able, they set off for Worms to find a surgeon and rest until their wounds healed, but they dared not risk staying too long, and as soon as they were able to travel, set off for Aquitania.

"The first thing I will do when I get there is build up the Aquitani army," announced Waldere.

"Isn't there something else you should do first?" whispered Hagen, nodding towards Hildegund, who was regarding him with one of her scyldmæden pouts.

"After I have married my beloved, of course!" added Waldere.

The sun shone in Hildegund's face when she heard these words. Of course, she knew how much Waldere loved her, but martial matters had been so pressing of late, that she couldn't remember when he last kissed her – and she was looking forward to much more than kisses!

In Armorica

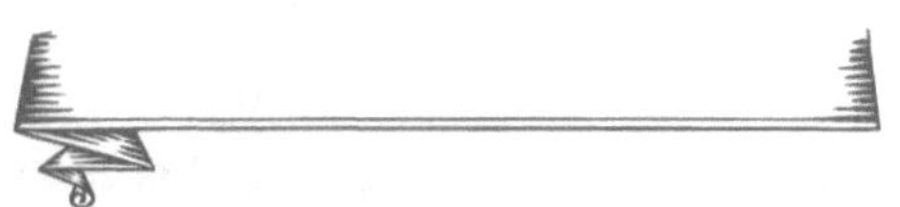

For Aurelius, the desperate flight from Britannia that he had suffered as a child was forgotten in the calm and quiet of the cloister. Despite pressure to become a military man, he had chosen the life of a lay brother in a monastery, not because he wished to be a monk, but because he loved learning. His brother, Uther, in contrast, delighted in military matters, and spent his time in building up a legion with which he hoped to win back Britannia – a vain hope in those days! His 'legion' was not much bigger than 500 men and few of them had proper arms and armour.

While Uther marched his toy legion on the parade ground, Aurelius liked nothing better than to sit in the scriptorium, the bright morning light streaming through the high window and illuminating the manuscript that he was reading or copying. It seemed he was transported though that manuscript, along the beam of sunlight, into another world: Paradise in the Old Testament, Bethlehem in the New, Ancient Greece, Ancient Rome, Gallia, when Caesar subdued it, Britannia, when Boudicca rebelled, or the legendary worlds of gods and heroes.

One day a wave of exclamation rippled the calm of this untroubled pool – and why? King Aldroenus had just walked into the scriptorium. The abbot hurried after him, rubbing his hands together anxiously. He looked around, recognised Aurelius and signalled that all the monks should leave the room at once, except him. The abbot ushered them out and soon the king and Aurelius were alone.

What could it be about? Usually, if Aldroenus wanted to speak to him, he'd send for him in his palace. It must be something of great importance to make him come in person. "My lord," said Aurelius, much bemused. "Could you not send for me as usual?"

The old king, his forehead lined with trouble, replied, "Just come with me. There's something that I want to show you."

He led Aurelius to the Roman barracks, his bodyguard following close behind. Uther was there, dressed in his finery as magister militum; a muscled cuirass and a jeweled parade helmet. He welcomed them with pleasure, and invited them to join him on the reviewing stand. "You're just in time. I'm going to put my legion through its paces – drill and close-order manoeuvering. I think you'll be impressed."

The drill consisted in marching in columns, then turning to the front, forming a shieldwall, and drawing and presenting swords. Aurelius was impressed at first. The front rank was well equipped in best Roman fashion, with ridge helmets and *lorica hamatae*,[6] javelins and swords of spatha type. Their shields bore the device of the red dragon, the ancient symbol of Britannia.

Uther noticed that Aurelius was looking at the symbol with some puzzlement and explained, "I call the legion, *Legio I Britannicus* in token of its purpose; to reconquer Britannia."

The old king said nothing, but looked hard at the young monk. Aurelius took the hint and a walked along the front rank, then the second and the third, and saw that every rank was less well equipped than the one in front of it. By the time he reached the rear ranks, the legionaries were legionaries no more, but ragged peasants with kitchen knives and pitchforks for their weapons.

He shook his head with disbelief: 500 men, a third of them poorly armed, and his brother called it a legion! He knew from his reading that an old Roman legion consisted of about 5,000 men, and that Caesar, when he invaded Gallia, had four legions, and by the time he had conquered, eight years later, he had as many as 11.

When he got back to the reviewing stand, the old king said, "What did you see, Aurelius?"

"My brother playing military games with toy soldiers. This so-called legion would not last a moment against a seasoned army half the size – and as for conquering Britannia!"

Uther fired up in his defence, "What do you know of military matters?"

"I've read the *De Re Militari* by Vegetius, and Caesar's *Gallic Wars*."

Uther just laughed. "You can't learn war from books! You need a sword, and men to practice with!"

Aurelius shook his head. "To begin with, you've nowhere near enough men."

"I'm halfway there!" protested Uther. "I might not be a bookworm like you, but I do know that Roman legions these days consist of around 1,000 men, not the 5,000 of former times."

"But a legion does not fight a battle by itself. It combines with other legions, auxiliaries, allies and foederati to create a field army, and in these uncertain times, the Roman field army is bigger than ever, maybe as large as 30,000 men."

Uther looked incredulous. "There aren't that many fighting men in the whole of Armorica! Anyway, we're not going to fight Attila, we're going to fight Vortigern, and you know as well as I do that Constantine stripped the country of its legions. What have they now? A few hundred trained legionaries and a few hundred mercenaries."

"Nevertheless, you need to double the size of your legion and recruit auxiliaries."

"What do you mean by auxiliaries?"

"Take *sagittarii*, archers, for example. How many do you have?"

Uther was flustered. "Well, none at the moment."

"And what of *equites*, cavalry?"

Now Uther smiled. "I have ten mounted men with special armour."

"Just ten? Well, what of artillery, *ballistae*, siege engines and the like?"

Uther was defensive. "There are none available. Except, perhaps in Rome."

"Attila has them. Any leader who is serious about war has them, otherwise his enemy can hold out in walled cities."

"Very well, I'll get hold of some somehow," Uther replied with a confident laugh. "What you see is just the beginning."

"And what about your logistics?"

"I run an army, not a logic school!"

It was Aurelius' turn to laugh. "I mean your plans for movement, storage and supply."

Uther was nonplussed. The king smiled sagely, then spoke in earnest tones to the two brothers. "Uther, I know you mean well, but this so called *Legio I Britannicus* of yours is just a toy legion. Perhaps, one day, it can be built up into a proper army."

Aurelius took up the king's message with more details: "You will need at least two legions, plus as many auxiliaries. Why don't you build up an auxiliary unit of Armorican archers? The Britons and the Armoricans have a particular skill with the bow which we could put to good use."

Uther liked the idea. "Now you're talking sense. I'll do that."

"Also, you need to make alliances, perhaps with Aquitania or Gallia."

"I'm not sure about that. I'm a man of action, not a diplomat."

Aldroenus shook his head in disagreement, "That's why you need to listen to Aurelius. He may not be a man of action, but he sees the bigger picture."

"Which is?" said Uther, not convinced.

"Strategy. In any case, Aurelius is the rightful king of Britannia, so Uther, you must follow his advice. Now, listen to my ruling: you will still be magister militum, but he, as future king, will be supreme commander."

"But he's a lay brother!"

"Not any more."

Aldroenus turned to Aurelius and said to him in a tone almost of regret: "Aurelius, I'm sorry, but you must leave the monastery and play your part as future king. I am long in years, and there is no other to succeed me, so you will be King of Armorica as well as King of Britannia – *Rex Britanniae* – King of the Britains, *Britannia Magna* and *Britannia Parva* as Romans call them."

Aurelius accepted that, as heir apparent, he would have to leave the cloister, but he felt that the idea of reconquering Britannia was a fool's dream. It had taken Claudius three legions to do it, and Armorica, a poor province at the end of the world, could barely raise one of the new type with only a thousand legionaries. He would do his duty, of course, but it was not how he had planned to spend his life. "What about my books?" he said sadly.

"Put them away for now, except for those that treat of training in the art of war – and get Uther to read them too. It sounds like he could do with a dose of Vegetius."

"Vegetables!" scoffed Uther. "It's raw beef for me, any day!"

"And that's what you will be if you don't listen to Aurelius: raw beef, chopped up and bloodied!"

Uther made his bow to the king, stamped down the steps of the reviewing stand, and disappeared into the barracks, leaving the king and Aurelius wondering what to do with the 500 men who stood expectantly before them.

A few days later, with a heavy heart, Aurelius left the cloister and shouldered the responsibility of his role: High King of Britannia, no, not yet! – *future* High King, something that would probably never happen – especially if it depended on that toy legion.

Fate Versus Free Will

In a few years the legion was transformed. Uther had built it up to a thousand men and most were well-equipped and well trained. He had also recruited auxiliaries who served as saggittarii and equites, though he still had no artillery. As an isolated region in what the Romans called *finis terre* – the end of the world – it was not easy to make alliances. Uther had hopes of the Aquitani. He had travelled to Burdigala in person, accompanied by the first minister, Judocus, and attempted to interest Ælfhere in an alliance: "Help us in the reconquest of Britannia and you will have a trading axis with two nations."

"What is Britannia to us?" said Ælfhere. "They call Armorica finis terre, do they not? So what is Britannia? *Inanis ultra* – the void beyond!"

"In any case," said Eawa, "you say we would be fighting Angles and Saxons. But they are as good as kin. The old sagas tell that we Visgoths came from Gothland, a near neighbor to Angeln and Saxony."

"Nevertheless," said Ælfhere, "we could do with an ally against Attila. What say you?"

Uther was nonplussed. He was a man of action and no diplomat, and now the tables had been turned. It was Judocus who saved the day: "Perhaps we can work out something of mutual advantage," he said. They talked for a lot longer, but that was how matters stood when Uther returned to Armorica.

Despite this disappointment, he was confident that his army of over 2,000 men, including the different auxiliary contingents, would be enough to take Britannia. "Think of the Britons who will flock to the banner of the rightful king!" he enthused.

But Aurelius was not so sure. Something was wrong somewhere, although he knew that everything he could do had been done. Their legion was well trained, and well equipped, and was the best disciplined in all of Gallia; as much like one of the old Roman legions as they could make it. So why should he worry? Numbers? They had over 2,000 men. But would it be enough? He had hoped to recruit more of those men who had fled from Britannia when Constantine had stripped the country bare of its defences, but most had forgotten their old home and were settled in Armorica. He had even appealed to Rome, but their magister militum, Aetius, replied that he had no men to spare as he was too busy defending the Empire, or what was left of it, against Attila.

It was hot night, sultry and oppressive. The brooding atmosphere matched his mood, seeming to confirm his doubts and fears. Perhaps he would rescind the marching order and try to enlarge his army by hiring Visigoth mercenaries – a bitter disappointment to his brother, and a blow to the morale of his men, but better that than military disaster.

Aurelius decided to go to bed, then rise early and ponder the matter when he was refreshed. Wearily, he climbed up to his chamber and threw himself onto his pallet bed. But he slept badly in the stifling heat, disturbed by thunderclaps which somehow found their way into his dream – an epic battle in which he led his mighty Roman legion against another, captained by his brother. Briton fought Briton, until finally all Britannia's manhood lay dead upon the field, leaving the realm to carrion crows and raiders.

He woke in a panic, screaming and pouring with sweat. As he came to himself and quietened down, he realised his doubts had crystallised; his dream had shown him what he feared – a civil war! Unless most Britons flocked to his banner, he would be setting Briton against Briton. Kinsmen would kill each other, but worse of all, they'd have no strength to fight Vortigern.

Aurelius drank some wine to clear his head. The storm had stopped, the darkness paled to dawn. He knew that he must make his mind up soon, but that bad dream didn't make it any easier. By now, it would be well nigh impossible to stop the momentum of his mighty project, and he would need decisiveness to do it.

He thought a walk might help to clear his thoughts, and went out quietly into the streets, being careful not to wake his sleeping household. He went in the direction of the forum, now a basilica; a Christian church. He entered the cool vastness of the building. A light was burning in the sanctuary, marking the place where the Host was reserved. Before he knew it, he was on his knees and praying fervently for a solution. Christ, who was crucified for the world's sins, might offer help to him, a humble sinner – but the solution did not come from Christ, rather a servant of older gods.

A figure strode towards him in the darkness, causing him to stand up in mild alarm. The man pulled back his hood to show his face, held his hands out to show that he was unarmed, and smiled to show that he came in a spirit of good will. His eyes were piercing and shone with wisdom, though of a different sort to the philosophers, and different also from the monks and priests. Aurelius thought he knew that face but couldn't place it. He'd seen those bright, far-seeing eyes before.

"I'm Merlin," said the man. "Don't you remember? I brought you and your brother from Britannia when that proud tyrant, Vortigern, killed Constans."

"Merlin!" he answered, suddenly remembering. "Why did you wait so many years to come? And why come in the middle of the night!"

"Many years to you, perhaps," smiled Merlin, "but not to me, for Time is an illusion: everything that has every happened and will happen in the future is already there, but mankind is only allowed to see it a bit at a time. As for the early hour, I come in secret."

Aurelius was still more mystified. "What secret? What have you to hide?"

"I know what has been troubling you," said Merlin, "and also know the answer to your question."

"How can you know?" replied Aurelius. "It was only last night I thought of it."

"I am not a man like you – I am a prophet."

"You mean, like Jeremiah in the Bible?"

"Yes, in a way, though my god is THE ONE. My duty is the guardianship of Albion, or Britannia, as they call the land today."

"But what has all this this got to do with me?"

"The present age is the Dark Age of Albion," continued Merlin. "Ruled by the Dark Lord, Vortigern, usurper, murderer, adulterer, idolater and more. Albion is falling into chaos – raids by Picts and Scots, Angles and Saxons, poverty, plague and civil strife!"

Aurelius looked up sharply and met his gaze.

"Yes," repeated Merlin: "Civil strife! Unless all Britons rally round one standard. That standard must be yours, Aurelius!"

"But how?" Aurelius said, daring to hope.

"With the aid of the fabled Sword of Albion!"

Aurelius' love of logic was offended; the Sword of Albion was just an ancient old-wives tale, not something you could use to lead a legion.

Merlin went on: "The Sword of Albion was won by Brutus, your first ancestor, who took it from a giant of that name and it became a symbol of the kingship."

"It's just a story – it doesn't exist!"

"It does exist – and you are going to find it, and then all Britons will acknowledge you as their rightful king."

"Where will I find this sword?" Aurelius said.

Merlin frowned. "I cannot help you there. I have already tried a finding spell, but whoever hid it hid it well. It is concealed by a far greater power."

This was too much for poor Aurelius. He waved his arms to wave the thing away: "You mean you expect me to scour Britannia to find a sword that has been so well hidden that even the great Merlin cannot find it!"

Merlin knew that the logically-minded Aurelius would take some convincing, so he tried again to explain it: "There are more powers than magic in the world and you are fortunate to have two in your favour. One – you are a learned scholar, a logician; two – you're fated to be Britannia's future king."

Aurelius smiled, for as a trained logician he was familiar with the old debate: Fate Versus Free Will. "The very fact that I'm a scholar makes me dubious that everything is somehow predetermined."

"Everything is written in the stars, where every opposition and conjunction is predetermined to the end of time. But I'm not here to play at rhetoric. I came to help."

This was not how Aurelius had been taught to argue, but there was something about Merlin that transcended Aristotle's syllogistic logic, so he conceded the point and said, "Then tell me what to do."

"You must examine all the manuscripts left in the cloister by your bother, Constans. He was a scholar like you, and your minds therefore have a similar cast, so if he hid the sword, and left a clue, you are more likely to spot it than I am."

"Why Constans?"

"He was the last anointed king of Britannia and must have known about the Sword of Albion."

That at least made sense. "But as for what you said about the stars, I can't believe that they control our fate."

Merlin sighed, "Put it another way. The fate of Albion is in the *Song of Albion*, sung by the seeress to lull the giant at the dawn of time. The sword is there, and so are you, Aurelius, and so am I, and all the past and future."

"So will I find the sword? Does it say that?"

"You will. But only if you look for it!"

Aurelius frowned. What sort of convoluted logic was this? If everything was fated, then he was fated to find the sword, whether he looked for it or not. Nevertheless, there was something convincing in Merlin's explanation, so he decided to go along with it: "Where must I look?"

"We'll make a start as soon as we can get to Britannia. We must plan our journey carefully – we have many enemies there! We'll go disguised as monks to Constans' cloister and get permission to look at his books. But mind – I have no knowledge of the Bible, or monkish ways. You'll have to cover for me."

Aurelius smiled. The thought of the great Merlin relying on him was a strange reversal.

"There's one more thing," said Merlin.

"What is that?"

"You must put off your plans for an invasion."

Sword of Albion

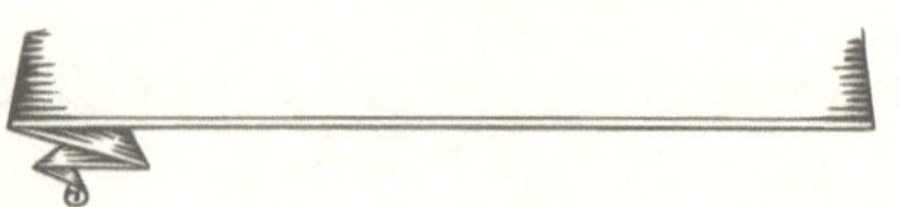

Two hooded figures leading well-packed mules arrived at Venta's[7] Cloister-House one night. The elder of the two was tall and gaunt, and well-advanced in years, needing the support of an unusually large and knobbly staff. He was wearing a monk's habit with an large cowl which cast the upper part of his face into shadow. His young companion was a lay brother, a novice, still in the monastic school, judging by his white robes.

At the gatehouse they were challenged by a warden wearing an incongruous combination of Roman armour and monkish habit: "Who are you, and what is it you want?" he said, suspiciously, for in those uncertain times you couldn't be too careful.

The younger answered, "We're monks from Condate Riedonum. We've been sent here to study by Abbot Marcus, our Father Superior. I am Brother Ambrosius, and my venerable companion is Brother Michael. He is working on a history of the world and wants to see what chronicles of Britannia are in your library. I am his assistant. Here is a letter from Abbot Marcus; there you'll see his seal."

The warden examined the letter, but could make nothing of it, his Latin being none of the best. Still, it looked authentic, so he took the letter to the abbot who seemed satisfied with it and told him to admit the visitors. The abbot questioned them closely and satisfied himself that they were genuine: the young man spoke with zeal about his Order and the old man showed much knowledge of his subject; the letter and the seal confirmed his judgement. He turned to a lay brother and said, "Conduct our guests to the *hospitium* and see that they are given food and drink," then he turned back to the business in hand – or tried to, but he couldn't quite forget the old man's face; it looked familiar, yet he couldn't place it; old and wrinkled, covered with grey stubble, yet shaven as commanded by his Order, and on his head, grey hair and the round tonsure worn by men of the Church – and yet, and yet...he thought he'd seen a face of similar mien among the courtiers of Vortigern. Was this some plot, or his imagination? Nevertheless he thought it would be wise to inform Vortigern, and so he sent a brother to his palace with a message.

Next day the visitors went to the library and questioned the librarian about Constans. "Did he own any books?"

"He had just three," said the librarian, "a gospel and a book of history; also a psalter made at his command, illuminated in the Celtic manner."

"What happened to those books?"

"Why, they are here, back in the library, for as you know, a man of God takes vows of poverty, whatever his connections."

"May we see them?"

"I'll bring them right away, and hope they will contribute to your studies."

"These books are in your line," the elder said, passing the gospel and the illuminated psalter to Brother Ambrosius.

"This history, the *Song of Albion*, is better left to me. I know it well."

"What are we looking for?" the young monk said.

"A clue to help us find the Sword of Albion," was the whispered reply. "You know the legend. I'll repeat the verses as they are written in the *Song of Albion*:

A sword was forged

by dwarvish blacksmiths
for the Giant Albion
at the dawning of this country
before it was conquered by men.
So large it is that a two-handed
hilt was made for men to wield,
and on that hilt, five blood-red rubies
symbolise blood to be spilled
in five great wounds in the last battle
fought before the world grows old,
and on the blade a fiery legend
is inscribed in words of gold:
QUI HABET HOC GLADIUM
ALBIONIS REGNABO.

The original is in Old Brythonic, of course, in which the last two lines are:

YR HWN SYDD YN DAL
CLEDDYF ALBION
A FYDD BRENHINIAETH
Y WLAD YN DAL.

Brother Ambrosius knew little of Old Brythonic, but to him, Latin was almost a mother tongue, and he translated the lines into Common Brythonic, speaking them in awestruck tones: *"Whosoever wields this sword shall be the rightful king of Albion."*

"Thus if we find the Sword of Albion, thousand of Britons will flock to our banner, like migratory birds that were lost but have found their way at last. Constans had that sword last, then it was lost. I think he hid it well, but left a clue, so search his books for notes and underlinings – anything out of the ordinary."

While they were poring over Constans' books, two voluminously cowled figures came into the room and watched them for awhile, then went away. The hours passed by, the sun achieved its zenith, a bell was heard, and the librarian suggested that they left their task awhile to join the brothers in their noonday service.

The cowled men were not monks, but servants of Vortigern, Picts by the names of Gart and Eog. They hurried to his palace with the news. "The stranger that the abbot thought suspicious is Merlin," said Gart, "though we were not sure at first. He's shaved his beard and wears the Roman tonsure, but he can't hide that beaky nose."

"The voice was Merlin's, I am certain," said Eog.

"Wait here for further orders," said the king, and went to tell Severa of the news. Latterly, it seemed that, though he styled himself imperator, he could take no important decision without consulting her.

"Kill him!" she cried, "while he is in your power." She said this without compunction for, as she got older, she got more severe and thought only of her own aggrandisement.

Vortigern, on the other hand, still had a few residual drops of the milk of human kindness: "He's just an old man. What good would it do? The danger's in Aurelius and Uther."

"Was it not he who saved them? Take revenge on that old mischief-maker. If you don't, he'll only do more harm. Why is he here? Spying, no doubt, to find our weaknesses!"

"What can he find out in a monastery?"

Severa pursed her lips with determination. "I've no idea, but let us take no chances. Order him killed today! Be resolute! If you had heeded me before there'd be no need, because the threat of Uther and Aurelius would not exist, but now we live in fear. So do it – put an end to that old meddler!"

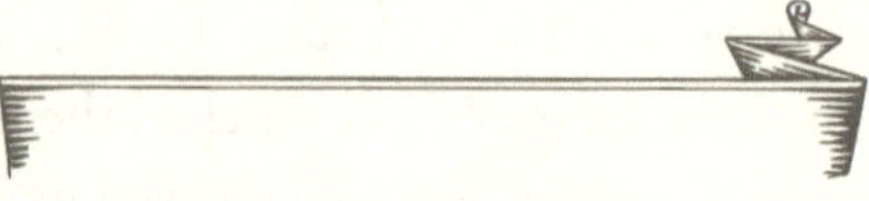

A Frail Old Man

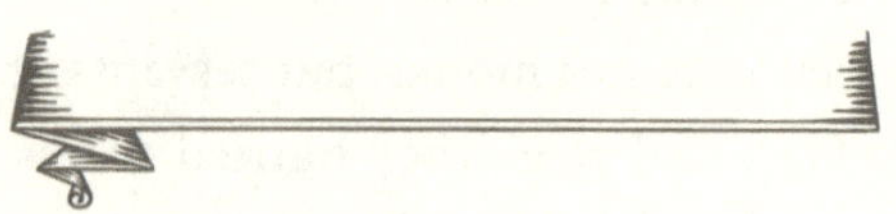

That afternoon they worked in the same way: the work was hard – the books had many glosses; notes translating Latin to Brythonic, cross-references and spiritual reflections, all of which had to be read and sifted.

At long last Merlin said: "I've found something written in the margin near those lines about the Sword of Albion where it says: 'He defeated all the giants, taking the mighty sword of one, which he called the Sword of Albion, to be a symbol of his kingship...' Next to it someone wrote: 'Psalm 149.'"

Brother Ambrosius found the page in the illuminated psalter and read the psalm. This is what he found:

> 6. Let the high praises of God be in their mouth; and a two-edged sword in their hand;

> 7. The sword is in a rocky place in Logres; across a river, hung between two ogres,

> 8. to execute vengeance upon the heathen; and punishments upon the people...

He looked at it with doubt, and read again.
"What is it?" questioned Merlin. "Tell me quickly!"
"The psalm is wrong! Verse 7 should not be there!"
"Read it out loud!" cried Merlin eagerly.

"The sword is in a rocky place in Logres; across a river, hung between two ogres."

"How do you know verse 7 should not be there? Do you know the psalter so well."

"We chant from the psalter six times a day in the daily offices. In any case, Logres is the ancient name for part of this island, but The Bible never mentions this country at all. It was of no importance in Biblical times, just a heart of darkness at the edge of the world."

"That's it, then!" said Merlin. "That's what we have been seeking!"

Brother Ambrosius looked perplexed. "It makes no sense."

"It does, in a way. Look how it continues: 'to execute vengeance upon the heathen; and punishments upon the people' – that's the Cerebos-worshipping Vortigern and his druids and mercenaries, the Picts and the Saxons."

"But it doesn't tell us where to look," objected Aurelius.

"Because it is a riddle," Merlin said. "Constans couldn't write the message clearly because it might fall into evil hands. Show me the text."

Merlin read the words over and over again, screwed up his features in thought, rubbed his brow, pulled his beard, then finally shook his head, "It's not easy – but I will work it out or I'm not Merlin!"

By then, the evening shadows began to fill the room and the librarian brought them a candle. "There is not long before the bell for Compline," he said, and the abbot has told me that he would be honoured if you would take part in the service.

"Thank you," Merlin replied. "We will be ready." Then turning to Brother Ambrosius, he said with a note of urgency: "Memorise these lines and leave at once. Oh, and take my staff. It's a good one and I don't want to lose it."

"But aren't you coming with me?"

"Alas, no! There is much more sung in the *Song of Albion* than has ever been written down on parchment. My time has come. Vortigern knows I'm here, and I must be the sacrifice that takes his eyes from you so you can keep the secret; the riddle that will lead you to the sword, and thus restore Britannia's rightful king. You must go now; the Compline bell is ringing and Vortigern's men are near. Farewell, Aurelius."

Realising that he had just spoken the young monk's real name aloud, he winced and put a finger to his lips, but looking round, he saw with relief that there was no-one near enough to hear him. "Go now! Leave with the other monks, but don't go to the service. Leave by the back way."

Brother Ambrosius opened his mouth to protest, but Merlin silenced him with a finger across his lips. Aurelius could see from the expression on his face that matters were serious and that he must obey him implicitly, so he left with the other monks, while Merlin waited for the coming doom.

The candle flickered, casting gloomy shadows; shadows of two cowled men, which loomed above him in the dim light like two giants. They reached inside their robes and drew their daggers. "Prepare to die," said Gart, "on the king's orders."

"You can't kill me!" said Merlin, rising quickly, and hurrying to the doorway of the library.

They hesitated for a moment, perhaps thinking of Merlin's reputation as a mighty mage, and fearing what he might do to them. Indeed, if he had faced them down, they might have fled, but Vortigern had promised them rich rewards, and had chosen them because they were hard-bitten brutes with little imagination. Gart steeled his nerve and replied, "Oh yes we can!" and strode across the room to cut off his retreat. Eog went behind and thrust his blade into his back. Then Gart finished him off with a blade in his belly, and the blood gushed out, staining the dark brown habit. Merlin fell, and lay unmoving in a pool of blood.

"Ha!" said the Gart, "there he lies – dead! A fool who told us that we couldn't kill him!"

"Yes," said Eog, "and without a fight. They said he was a wizard – where's his magic?"

"Wizard indeed! Only a frail old man!"

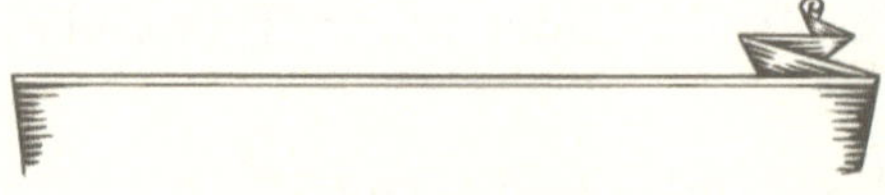

The Empire Pleads for Help

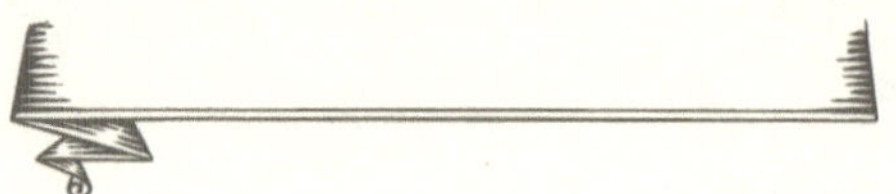

Brother Ambrosius hurried to the stables to find his mule. It was late, and the stable boy was already asleep, curled up in the hay beside the horses. "Wake up!" he said, shaking him roughly. The boy sat up and rubbed the sleep out of his eyes.

"Quickly!" urged Brother Ambrosius. "Saddle my mule!" As he said these words, the stable boy lit an oil lamp, and Brother Ambrosius scanned the stalls looking for his mule. His eyes stopped on a magnificent black horse of the finest Libyan breed. "Never mind that," he said to the boy, who was leading out his mule. "I'll take that one."

"But that's the abbot's," objected the boy.

"Nevertheless, you'll do as I say," said Brother Ambrosius, "and while you're at it, you'll give me your clothes."

The boy gawped at him as though he were a madman.

"Do it!" snapped Brother Ambrosius, "before you find out the hard way who I really am!" and with these words he flourished Merlin's staff. The gesture was enough, and the boy fell to work on the abbot's horse. Ambrosius helped him, and within minutes he was leading the horse out of the gate dressed as a stable boy, accompanied by the stable boy dressed as a monk. The warden, seeing nothing out of the ordinary, let them pass.

A moment later, a cry was heard from the Cloister House steps: "Bar the gate! Let no-one out!"

But the warden, who thought he knew all the monks by sight, did not recognise Vortigern's men and decided to play safe: "Who are you, and what is your authority?" he said.

One of the men threw back his hood and said, "Men of the king's bodyguard. Now, obey my order before it is too late!"

"Who are you trying to stop?" said the door-ward. "They are all at Compline."

"A young monk. A visitor to the abbey."

"Then you're too late. He's gone already."

"Fool!" roared the man, then turning to his companion, he said, "Come on! Hurry up! We can still catch him, then we'll kill him according to orders!"

They hurried out into the street, and questioned an old man, whom they found sitting near the abbey gate begging for alms.

"Did you see a young monk, just now?" said the guard.

"Yes, my lord. Give alms."

"Which way did he go?"

"That way, my lord. Give alms."

"Here are your alms!" said the guard and kicked him. The other guard followed suit and the two of them ran down the road the beggar had indicated. Had they questioned him more closely, and been kinder to him, they might have learned that another man had left the abbey and galloped off in the opposite direction. But Brother Ambrosius, now Aurelius again, had threatened the stable boy and told him which way to run. The boy, glad of the chance of escaping this dangerous visitor, had been only too glad to comply. It did not take the guards long to catch up with the boy and find out their mistake, but by then, Aurelius was well on the way to Londonium where he planned to take ship to Osismis.[8]

In Osismis, Aurelius found refuge in the monastery where he was given a new habit and become Brother Ambrosius again. From there, it was only a day's journey to Ludia, which he made in the company of a brotherhood of monks who were visiting his old monastery. Another day's journey took him to Riedonum.

How pleasant it was to see the distinctive red brick walls of the city; home at last! He had only just dismounted, tired and travel-weary, and looking forward to refreshment in the hospitium, when he was approached by a messenger from his brother. The messenger seemed to be in hurry and there was an anxious look in his eyes. He made his bow, then rapped out his message: "My lord, Uther, requests your immediate presence in the palace on an urgent affair of state!"

"How does he know I am here?"

"News travels fast my lord, and monks are slow."

Brother Ambrosius realized that he was Aurelius once again and must prepare himself to take up the cares of kingship-in-waiting. He sighed. "How urgent? Can he wait until I have taken some refreshment."

"My lord," said the servant, nervously. "He has been fretting over this matter for days, and I believe he would wish you to come at once."

Aurelius sighed again and climbed back onto his mule.

"No need," said the messenger. "My lord, Uther, has sent an escort."

At that moment, two cavalrymen on fine horses, leading his own horse, *Achilles*, clattered into the courtyard. Aurelius welcomed *Achilles* like an old friend, patted his muzzle, and climbed into the saddle. He had no time to change his clothes, and laughed to himself as he thought what an incongruous sight he would be to the people – a poor, travel-stained monk on a horse fit for a king.

He found his brother pacing up and down in the audience chamber of the royal apartments. Uther turned round at the sound of footsteps, and hurried to embrace him. "At last!" he said, sounding much relieved. "I thought you would never come! There is an urgent matter..."

"But don't you want to hear about..." began Aurelius, thinking that nothing could be more important than his tragic news about Merlin's death.

"Later, later..." said Uther, consumed with the urgency of his own problem. "There's a messenger from Flavius Aetius, and he won't go away. I keep telling him he is wasting his time, but he won't take no for an answer. He's an important man, the Praetorian Prefect of Gallia, so we mustn't keep him waiting any longer. But it's better if you deal with him. I'm no diplomat. I am a man of action. In any case, it's your decision. You are the future king."

"But what is it all about?" said Aurelius.

"It will ruin all our plans," said Uther, not making the matter any clearer.

Aurelius realised he would get nowhere with Uther while he was in this excitable mood, so he decided to get to the heart of the matter himself.

"I will see this messenger..."

Uther breathed an audible sigh of relief.

"But not now, and not like this. I need to eat, drink, rest, and change these robes, and then I can meet him as heir to throne, and not as a lowly lay brother – and while I'm changing, I want you to listen to my news."

Uther followed him to his private apartment, aware, now that his own troubles had been blurted out, that his brother was the bearer of bad tidings. Aurelius explained what had happened, simply, clearly, and without betraying his emotion. But Uther saw the emotion beneath the surface and quite forgot about his troublesome messenger – a problem which seemed trivial by comparison with his brother's grief. "So you think Merlin is dead?" he said, after he had digested his brother's story.

"He spoke of being a 'sacrifice'. I think he knew that Vortigern had sent men to kill us, and he wanted to give me time to get away."

"So he gave his life to save yours?"

"And the secret of the sword," said Aurelius. Then, to take the sting out of his news he mentioned a thought with which he had sometimes consoled himself: "Merlin might have got away, after all. He said he was a wizard. I find it hard to believe in such things, but he did seem to have remarkable powers."

Uther looked puzzled, and Aurelius realised that Uther hardly knew Merlin, and did not feel the loss in the same way. "Did you find what you were looking for?" said Uther.

"I don't know – a few cryptic words. A clue, perhaps. But it's not much use without Merlin's help to interpret it." Aurelius stopped speaking as emotion over-whelmed him – sorrow for the death of Merlin, regret for the lost hope of the Sword of Albion. Uther saw his sorrow and said grimly, "It only stiffens my resolve to march on that usurper!"

"Without the sword?" said Aurelius.

"I never really believed in the sword," he said. "It's just an old story. I believe in what I can see and touch – in other words in the swords and spears of my legion."

Aurelius decided that this was not the time to remind Uther that his legion was still nothing like a real Roman legion, or to wallow in regret about what had happened in Venta. Instead, he decided it was time to turn his attention to affairs of state. "Now, about this messenger..."

Uther and Aurelius arranged themselves in state in the throne room of palace, and the messenger was shown in. Ambrosius saw at once that he was a Roman officer of high rank, very high rank if he was the Prefect of Gallia. The guard announced him as Eparchius Avitus, and the name sounded familiar.

Avitus stood before the throne and gave the Roman salute. Then, addressing Uther, he spoke: "Thank you, my lord, for agreeing to hear me again."

Uther replied, relieved to pass the matter on: "My brother, Aurelius Ambrosius, heir to the throne of Armorica and Britannia, has returned from his journey and will hear your petition."

"Here is the message in Aetius' own words and with his seal," said Avitus, holding out a scroll.

Aurelius took the scroll, looked at it and said, "Please summarise it in your own words."

"It is simply this: the west is threatened by Attila. Aetius requests that you join your forces with his and fight for Rome."

Despite the fact that Uther had handed the matter to his brother, he could not hide his exasperation, or refrain from intervening. "Armorica has not been part of the Empire since the time of my father, Constantine the Fair. Why should we fight for Rome?"

Avitus looked from one to the other as though he wondered whom he was dealing with. Aurelius, with his usual quiet authority, took charge again, "It is a fair point. How would you answer it?"

Avitus gathered his thoughts, perhaps wondering which were the best arguments to impress his hearers. "You will not be fighting for Rome, but for yourselves. If Attila takes Gallia, Armorica is next."

"Then, perhaps, will be the time to deploy our legion," said Aurelius.

Avitus gathered his thoughts again. "You have heard the old saying, 'United we stand; divided we fall' – well, the whole of the west is uniting against Attila: Salian Franks, Ripuarian Franks, Sarmatians, Liticians, Saxons, and many other Celtic and German tribes. When I have finished here, and hopefully won your support, I am going to Ælfhere, king of the Aquitani, then Theodoric, king of the Visigoths, then Hereric, king of Burgundia. If they all agree to join Aetius we will have a mighty army indeed, and believe me, Aetius needs every man.

His own legions are but a shadow of the legions of the past, a shambles of foederati, auxiliaries and new recruits with scarcely a Roman citizen among them."

Aurelius had heard of this alliance, but it still gave him pause for thought, "As I have already told you," he said slowly, weighing his words, "my legion has been created to reconquer Britannia. When that task is achieved, I may consider sending part of it to join Aetius."

"By then it will be too late," said the Avitus. "Attila has already crossed the Rhine and laid siege to Divodurum. The last I heard, he was besieging Aurelianum[9] – probably by now it has fallen."

Aurelius looked up with surprise. This latest piece of news had struck home. Aurelianum was not far from Armorica's eastern border. He said something in a low voice to Uther, then held up his hand to signal that the audience had come to an end. "We will debate this matter in council and you will have our answer by tomorrow."

Avitus bowed and took his leave. Uther, with whom diplomacy was never a strong point, called after him: "Our final answer!"

Aurelius and Uther were just about to discuss the interview when the guard reminded him that another petitioner was waiting. It was Judocus. Aurelius gave the word to admit him. Judocus was first minister and saw to the administration of the decisions taken by those above him, as well as having some influence on them himself. He was a young, earnest man, who could sometimes be irritating in his manner, but who had the well-being of the Armorican people close to his heart.

"It is about the matter of taxes, my lord," he began.

Aurelius felt angry, though schooled himself not to reveal it. He knew that Judocus meant well, but felt that it was not the time to raise such a routine matter. Nevertheless, he thought it best to hear him: "Go on," he said..

"Taxes have doubled in the last three years. The burden is unsustainable. What need has a small country like Armorica of a legion such as..."

Aurelius cut him short with one word, "Attila."

Of course, Judocus had heard about the threat from Attila, but it seemed so distant – something that concerned Rome and its empire, and Armorica had long since seceded from the Empire. "Attila is..."

"Snapping at our heels. The latest news is that he is besieging Aurelianum. If it falls..." Even as he said the words, Aurelius was surprised to find himself repeating Avitus' arguments – and they seemed surprisingly effective: Judocus did not need to have the consequences spelled out, he merely bowed in submission and turned to go. He was still concerned about the tax burden, and resolved to raise the matter again when circumstances were more favourable.

As soon as he had left the room, Aurelius dismissed the guards and said, "We don't need to call the council to discuss Aetius' petition. It is clear enough what we must do – as you could see just now – we must postpone our planned invasion."

Uther protested strongly: "But why? This is the second time. I thought you agreed with me!"

"We have to fight to stop the Hun. If we don't, there'll be no Armorica. What is the point of gaining a kingdom, if you lose another at the same time? And there's no guarantee that we can defeat Vortigern. We might end up with nothing."

"But think of the risk to our legion!" Uther spluttered.

"If Attila defeats Aetius and conquers Gallia, we will be next."

"We've been building up our legion to reconquer Britannia!"

"If we made the attempt, we would be leaving our people at the mercy of Attila. But there is one other thing. I know you are proud of our legion, but in my opinion it is still unequal to the task of conquering Britannia. Despite our efforts, it is still under strength."

"But you were ready enough to reconquer Britannia until Merlin fuddled your mind with all that nonsense about the Sword of Albion."

Aurelius shook his head. "I had my doubts but I never told you about them. I had a sleepless night because I was worrying about whether we had enough men, I went out to clear my head, and it was then that I met Merlin."

"But our legion is 2,000 strong and growing!"

"That's just it, Uther. You think 2,000 is lot. But believe me, I have studied Roman history, and I can tell you that the Gallic field army, in the days when it was up to full strength, numbered around 40,000 men."

"But that was in the heyday of Empire! What has Rome now?"

"Even in these straightened times, Aetius is building an alliance that will be 20 or 30,000 strong. Oh, it will not be like the Gallic field army, manned by citizen legionaries. Today's legionaries are a shadow of the past: underpaid, sometimes not paid at all, and not so well-armed or trained; and there are so few of them. The bulk of Aetius' field army will be made up of auxiliaries, foederati and allies. But why not join Aetius and find out? Look at it like this. Our legion will gain fighting experience, and we can both learn from watching the field army at work, and from Aetius himself. You have heard, no doubt, that he is feted as one of Rome's greatest generals. Some even compare him to the great Stilicho!"

Uther looked interested, and his stubborn expression began to soften. "Perhaps you're right," he said after a long, thoughtful silence. "Send for Avitus."

Home at Last

What does the exile feel when he comes home? It is as though the years in exile are wiped away at a stroke. The sights and sounds of that half forgotten landscape become familiar again, the very voices of the ordinary people speaking, not just your language, but your dialect with the self-same intonation – all these can move a strong man to tears, especially one who has suffered much. News of Waldere's arrival travelled before him, so that the great gates of Burdigala were thrown open to great him, and cheering crowds thronged their humble train – two horses, and a wagon for Gunther and Hildegund. Waldere acknowledged their greetings by waving his good left hand, and looked forward to seeing his old friends, and his father, Ælfhere, within.

The great gates were closed behind them, and Waldere looked round wondering where the welcoming crowds were. All he could see was a contingent of armed guards. While he was trying to make sense of this unexpected welcome, their captain stepped forward and ordered, "Arrest them!" and moments later, they were being hustled unceremoniously towards the guardhouse, which was to serve as a prison for the three men. Hildegund was taken somewhere else.

"Do you know who I am?" said Waldere, burning with indignation.

The guards ignored him.

"I am Waldere, son of Ælfhere, and I demand to see my father!"

"You have been arrested on the king's orders," said the captain.

"Impossible!" screamed Waldere. "What father would arrest his own son? There has been some mistake. I demand to see him."

But the captain ignored him and turned to leave the guardhouse.

"Wait!" called Gunther. "You have no right to detain me! I am Gunther, son of Gibicho, king of the Franks. If you do not release me immediately, you will have the Frankish army to answer to!"

The captain seemed to take notice of this. He hesitated for a moment, then sent a subordinate to bring a man of higher authority. Moments later, Malrede entered the guardhouse.

"Ah, Malrede," said Waldere with a sigh of relief. "Now we can talk sense. There has been a misunderstanding, so order our release."

Malrede sighed, as if with deep regret, and said, "That I cannot do. You are here on the king's orders..."

"But..."

"Attila's envoys have threatened reprisals if you are not returned to Pannonia.[10] The king has no choice."

"We must fight Attila. An alliance is forming against him with Aetius at its head. We must join that!"

"My lord, I am sure you remember our discussions in the council. There were many voices raised in favour of fighting Attila, but in the end we had no choice but to sue for peace. Nothing has changed."

"Let me see my father, at least."

"That I cannot do," said Malrede. "In any case, I am not here to discuss your case – the king's word on that is final – but to see about the man who claims to be king of the Franks."

"That's me!" said Gunther. "I was Attila's hostage, too, but I was given permission to leave Pannonia, so if you detain me you will have to answer to him as well as to the Frankish army."

Malrede had no oily words to slither out of this one, and the diplomat in him saw that he must act at once. "If you are who you say you are, you will be released."

"Here is my seal. Hagen, here, is my kinsman, and Waldere and Hildegund know me of old. They will vouch for my identity."

"It is enough," said Malrede. "You are free to go – though you do not look well enough to travel."

The long journey over bad roads had opened Gunther's wound again, and the bandage round the stump was wet with blood.

"I'll do well enough," said Gunther.

"Nevertheless," said Malrede, "I will send you to more comfortable quarters and ask the king's own physician to attend you."

Gunther suspected it would be nothing more than a more comfortable prison, but his wound gave him no choice but to accept.

"What of Hildegund?" said Waldere.

"She, also, is an escaped hostage, and must be returned."

"But King Ælfhere has no authority to decide that. Only her father, King Hereric, can make that decision."

"King Hereric has been consulted," replied Malrede, "and he is of the same opinion."

But the lie was too glib. How could King Hereric know that his daughter had arrived in Aquitania?

"My father should be careful about how he disposes of Hereric's beloved daughter. The Burgundians might not be able to do much against Attila, but they could put up a brave show against the Aquitani!"

Malrede's eyes shifted this way and that – the point had struck home – but, recovering himself, he said, "Nevertheless, I have my orders. We will depart tomorrow morning with a guard of 100 men, and I will, myself personally, escort you to Attila."

"With the expectation of a rich reward," said Waldere.

Malrede kept his stony-faced expression. "Doing my duty is reward enough," he said, and, turning his back to show that the interview was over, left the guardhouse.

As soon as the door was shut and barred, Waldere said, "This is Malrede's work. He was always a bad influence, and it seems he has managed to get complete control over my father. If only I could speak to him myself."

Hagen was looking around, trying to find a weak spot in the guardhouse through which they might escape. "Help me," he said, "I can't see as well as I used to!"

But it was no use. There were small, high windows to the inner wall, but they were too small to squeeze through. The walls were of stone and the only door was made of heavy planks of wood and was barred on the outside.

"Never mind," said Hagen. "It is a long way to Pannonia, and if we watch and wait, our chance will come."

They passed the afternoon making plans for their escape. Waldere refused to give in to the cloud of despondency that hung over them. "We have come through worse than this," he said, "so let's keep our spirits up!"

As evening came on, the guardroom began to darken, and they wondered if their guard was going to bring light and food. A scraping on the door raised their hopes. It was probably their guard removing the bars. But it wasn't the guard. It was a stranger, cloaked and hooded. He pushed back his hood, and they saw the friendly face and grizzled beard of Eawa.

"It is a poor welcome we have given you, Waldere," he said. "I dared not come earlier, and even now, I come without authority."

"It's good to see you," Waldere, holding out his left hand. Eawa saw the stump of his right hand, but said nothing, and shook his left hand warmly. "By the way, this is Hagen, a good friend of mine who shared my captivity."

"Aquitani hospitality is usually a good deal better than this," said Eawa ruefully.

"But can you help us?" said Waldere.

"As I said, I come without authority."

"But you are a member of the king's council; one of his most trusted advisers."

"Was. There is no council now – except for Malrede's place-men. Since you left, he insinuated himself more and more into the Ælfhere's favour and filled his head with bad advice. He started a whispering campaign against me, Graf, and his other loyal counsellors, until, one by one, we were dismissed. Now he has complete control over the king, and to make matters worse, Ælfhere is getting old. He was always – if you will forgive me for being frank – a ditherer, but his mind became more and more feeble, and Malrede took advantage of it. He heard about the fabulous wealth that Attila offered to anyone who could return Waldere to him, and he was determined to win it. All he had to do was to persuade Ælfhere that Attila would raze his city to the ground if he didn't return you according to the treaty."

"Is there nothing you can do?"

"Nothing at the moment. I cannot even get to see the king, and if I am not careful I will find myself locked in here with you. But I have an idea – just the inkling of one – so I can't say much about it just now. Put it like this: it's a long way to Pannonia."

"That's just what I said," said Hagen.

"And you have many loyal friends in Aquitania."

"I hope so," said Waldere.

"And Aetius is building an alliance."

"We have heard of it," said Hagen.

"And the Burgundians might have something to say about Hildegund."

"That's what I said to Malrede," said Waldere.

"And your friend, Gunther, might also have something to say.'"

"But he is unable to travel."

"Indeed, but the time will come."

"What I am saying is that these are pieces in a puzzle, but I am not sure how best to put them together."

"What shall we do, then?"

"Go along with Malrede and watch and wait. He doesn't know it yet, but he is making a big mistake in leading the party himself. Of course, he wants to make sure of his reward, but with him out of the way, I – along with Graf and the others – will soon outmanouvre Malrede's place-men, and then...well, we'll see what can be done."

The door opened. It was the guard bringing food and light. "I must go. May God be with you Waldere; and, Hagen, I hope that next time we meet it will be with the best of Aquitani hospitality!"

The Advantage of No Hand

They were awoken before dawn and made ready for the journey. They were mounted on horseback with their hands – in Waldere's case, hand – tied behind their backs, and their legs tied to the girth; a guard was given the task of leading each horse by the reins. Waldere was relieved to find that they had been given their own horses, his faithful *Lion* and Hagen's *Lightening*. That would help considerably when it came to making their break, as Malrede had no idea of the union between a Hunnic horseman and his horse. Hildegund was to travel in the wagon. Waldere soon realised that the reason for the early start was to avoid trouble from the crowd. Even so, a fair number of people had gathered to protest at so hurried a departure, and to jeer at Malrede, whom they suspected – quite rightly – of returning Waldere to Attila. As they rode away from the city, Waldere turned round for one last look, and there, on the parapet of the gatehouse, was a grey-haired old man, waving frantically – it was his father, Ælfhere. His heart missed a beat to see how his father had fallen into feeble old age while he had been away, and all he could do now was raise his good hand and wave back.

Malrede deployed his guardsmen along the sides of the road and when Burdigala was well behind them, formed them into a protective column, half in front of the captives and half behind. It was slow going, as they could only travel at the pace of the wagon, which was heavily built and easily got bogged down when the travelled along the unpaved road that led to the Via Agrippa. From there, the going was easy along the well-made and still smooth road. Malrede had planned to follow the road to Lugdunum, then go straight on through Burgundia, but he had taken note of Waldere's warning about King Hereric, and decided that it would be safest to keep out of that country. So instead, he planned to leave the Via Agrippa at Ubium and work his way around it.

However, he never got that far. On the sixth day of their journey, just after leaving Fines, a scout reported a large army blocking the road in front of them. "Burgundians by their banner," said the scout, "bearing the device of a snared fox."

Word was passed down the ranks, and it was not long before Waldere and Hagen heard it, and Hildegund must have heard it too.

"It looks like Eawa got word to King Hereric," said Waldere. "We are saved!"

"Back!" Malrede passed the order. "Back to Fines. Then we take the road north."

The clumsy wagon was turned, and the cavalcade set off in the opposite direction, but they had not gone far, when the scouts reported another army. "It's our own people," said one.

"Fools!" screamed Malrede. The scouts thought he was referring to them, and one of them replied, "My lord, there is no mistake. They are Aquitani under the banner of the golden lion." But Malrede had been thinking of his place-men, and Eofor in particular, his right hand man. They were supposed to uphold his position in his absence, but he realised now that his power was personal and could not be wielded by proxy, and that he had made a big mistake in leaving Burdigala.

Nevertheless, he believed that quick thinking might save the situation. "Leave the wagon and the girl!" he ordered. "That should keep King Hereric happy! I want six men to come with me. The rest of you can act as a rearguard," and with those words, he led Waldere and Hagen off the road onto a narrow track leading north.

The two armies marched cautiously forwards, and found Malrede's bodyguard in disarray, not knowing which way to face. Grimwald, Ælfhere's grizzled war-chief, took the situation in hand by riding forward under a flag of truce.

"Men, you know me," he said, "and you know that I am as good as my word. Lay down your arms and rejoin Ælfhere's army, and no reprisals will be taken against you."

To a man, and without hesitation, they threw down their arms. Now that Malrede had left them they had no hope of the fabulous rewards he had promised them, neither had they any relish for taking up arms against former comrades.

"You will be taken under guard as a precaution, but when we get back to Burdigala you will be given your freedom. Now, let's see about catching that villain!" and he rode up and down his ranks giving orders about the pursuit.

Malrede's small party hurried forward on the narrow track. Waldere sensed that this was the time to make their move, while Malrede was disoriented and the Aquitani army was not far behind them. He warned Hagen with a few words in the Hunnic language, pretending to his guard that he was grumbling about the rocky trackway.

They came to a stream with a low hill on the opposite side, which looked like a promising place to put his plan into action. He hung back, controlling his horse with his knees, and Hagen did the same. Malrede, at the top of the hill, called after them: "Hurry up!" The two guards whipped their horses, but *Lion* and *Lightening* still delayed, obeying only their masters. By the time they had crossed the stream, the other four guards had got ahead, and the guards leading Waldere and Hagen were tugging at the reins. While this was happening, Waldere was working his right arm free, and it was easy, because there was no hand to stop his arm sliding out of the rope. With his right arm out of the way, the rope went slack and it was easy to free his left hand, but he kept it behind his back ready for his next move: he urged *Lion* forward with a press of his knees and in a moment was beside his guard. With his left hand, he reached out, unsheathed the guard's *seax*, and sheathed it again – in his throat. The guard gave a half strangled gurgle and fell off his horse spluttering blood. Hagen's guard was quick to react. He drew his sword and charged towards Waldere, but Waldere made a move that he had practiced often with Attila: he leaned right over to one side of his horse in a position that would seem impossible to any Germanic horseman, and the sword missed him. Then he swung round and stabbed the guard in the back, though the guard's byrnie turned the thrust.

"Ride!" yelled Waldere, and the two of them rode as fast as they could in the direction of the Aquitani army, Waldere still tied by the girth and Hagen still with both hands tied behind his back, but they were used to controlling a horse with only their knees, so they were able to ride just as fast, indeed, faster than their pursuers. The track was rough, but that was no impediment to the sturdy Hunnic horses, and their pursuers fell further and further behind.

"The golden lion!" cried Waldere, pointing his stump towards the distant banner of the Aquitani. Malrede must have seen it too, for he turned quickly and galloped in the opposite direction.

Moments later, Waldere was being greeted by Grimwald, though they had no time to waste on the courtesies. Grimwald signalled to his men to continue the chase, sending separate detachments in different directions in case, as was likely, Maldrede had left the track and sought cover in the undergrowth. He left them to it, and gave himself the well-deserved honour of escorting the two men back to the Via Agrippa.

They found a large crowd gathered around the wagon, and in the middle of it, Hildegund in the arms of her father, sobbing her heart out. Hereric welcomed Waldere with a wry smile and the words, "It's a bit of a mess that you've got us all into!"

"It was my fault," said Hagen. "I was the first hostage to run away."

"You had no choice. Gunther broke the treaty," said Waldere.

"We've all broken the treaty now," said Hereric. "But, luckily, there is Aetius."

"What's the latest news?" said Waldere.

"Aetius' alliance grows by the day. He already has the support of the Visigoths and the Alans, and is negotiating with the Armoricans and the Franks even now. As for me..." here he gave a wry laugh. "I have no choice but to join him."

"We will join him too," said Waldere, already feeling his new responsibilities as heir apparent. Grimwald signalled his approval.

"Let's talk of happier things," said Hereric. "My daughter tells me that you have renewed the vows that your father and I made on your behalf when you were children. So be it! I am happy that the wedding is to take place at last. I will send my army home and accompany you with my house-troop to Burdigala, and we will tie the knot before any other upstart barbarian can get in the way!"

Waldere was welcomed home with more uproarious cheers than before – and there on the gatehouse was the old king, waving his hand again, but happily this time, in anticipation of seeing his long lost son. Later, he confessed his fault. "I feel better already now that Malrede is out of the way – but he was so convincing, everything he said seemed to make sense, even about sending you away – the treaty, Attila – and he advised me not to see you in case my heart got the better of my head. What happened to him, by the way?"

"He escaped. Even now he will be on his way to Attila."

"What sort of welcome do you think he'll get?"

"He'll be welcomed one way or another, because he knows a lot that will be of use to Attila – which of the kingdoms will side with him, which will be against him, and so on."

"How will he get it out of him?"

"It's hard to say. It might be the fist or it might be the glove..."

"Eh?"

"Either he'll be boiled alive like a lobster, or made much of...but Attila has a sense of honour, in his way, so my guess is that he'll be boiled alive for his traitorous act in trying to trick you."

"Ah well, as long as he is not bothering me, I don't care whether he is fried or feted. Now, about the wedding..."

"I think we should postpone that, father. Three vassal states have rebelled against Attila and if I know him he will not delay in seeking reprisals."

"But the campaigning season is over," said Hereric, "and, anyway, it is high time you two were married."

"I would not put too much trust in the season," said Waldere. "Attila moves quickly. He can move on Burgundia and be back in Pannonia again before the Alps become impassable."

"A quick wedding, and then to arms!" said Hereric.

"Agreed," said Ælfhere. "They have been betrothed long enough. If they were married next week nobody could say the business had been rushed."

Waldere smiled at the thought. It was what he wanted, after all, and Attila would not make any move until he knew for certain that the Burgundians and Aquitani had rebelled.

Marriage and Mimming

They were married in the basilica in Burdigala, now a Christian church. The Visigoths were Arian Christians – not that that made any difference to the ceremony, and not that anybody, except a few priests and scholars, could explain why it was different to Roman Christianity; it was something to do with the Trinity, but all that mattered to Waldere and Hildegund was that they were united at last, not in the Hunnic style, in which a wife was little better than a handmaid, but as equals before God,

Waldere's right hand was restored in the shape of a stuffed glove of buff leather, skillfully made with a natural curve so that it was hard to distinguish from a real hand, and Hildegund had a new kirtle made especially for the occasion, cut in Visigoth style, but made of silk imported from Cos.

After the service in the basilica, they had an informal handfasting under the Donar Oak just outside the city. That oak had been sacred for hundreds of years before the Romans came, and was called *The Duir* by the Celtic Aquitani tribe. The Romans had tolerated it, and the Arian Visigoths tolerated it too, referring to it as the Donar Oak in remembrance of one of their old gods.

That night, a great feast was held in which all of Burdigala took part, the lords in the hall, the burghers in leather tents, and the common folk at hastily improvised trestle tables in the open air. Toast followed toast until the guests could hardly stand, but Waldere was saving himself for the most important battle of his life; the battle of the bedroom, which he would have to fight without his preferred weapons in a delicious kind of unarmed combat. He was strong, he was trained in wrestling, but Hildegund gave as good as she got, and could have kept up the wrestling match for longer. Never mind, that wonderful Nordic custom called 'honeymoon' meant that they had nothing to do for the next month but drink mead and make babies – at least, that's what Hildegund was expecting. Imagine her surprise when, at break of day, Waldere rolled out of bed and started to dress.

"My love, where are you going?"

"I must pound the pell. I must make this hand as strong as my right hand used to be!"

"No!" she cried. "You must be ruled by me for once! You have work to do here! Pound me instead!" and with those words she pulled him back onto the bed with a takedown that would have impressed even Attila.

Hildegund thought that she was going to have her honeymoon after all, but before the week was out an important visitor was announced: Eparchius Avitus, Praetorian Prefect of Gallia, and Waldere was summoned to the council. Ælfhere had wisdom enough to know that his leadership could no longer be relied on, and, after his experience with Malrede, would trust no counsellors other than his son.

Avitus was delighted to find that King Hereric and King Gunther were also at the meeting. "That saves me much travelling!" he said, and then went into his explanation of the alliance that Aetius was building against Attila.

"This is music to our ears!" said Ælfhere.

"Indeed it is," agreed Hereric. "These young people..." he looked towards Hagen and Waldere, "...have got us into a pretty fix! We had no choice but to send them as hostages, but they fled – and what are we to do now? Our armies are no bigger than before!"

"But in the alliance..." said Avitus.

"What difference can our small armies make?" said Hereric.

"We must summon every man who is of military age," said Waldere. "The harvest is in, so they can be spared. We will train them as best we can."

"What about arms and armour?"

"Every blacksmith in Aquitania will be put to work!"

"That's the spirit!" said Avitus. "If every ally responded in the same way we would outnumber Attila ten to one!"

"I will see to it right away," said Waldere.

"But your honeymoon!" protested Hagen.

"I will make war by day and make love by night," laughed Waldere, "and when all this is over I will make it up to Hildegund in a very special way – perhaps with a trip to the Eternal City to bathe in the famous Baths of Caracalla."

"If it's still there!" said Avitus with a wry laugh.

"There is one more thing I must do to prepare for the coming conflict," said Waldere to Hildegund next morning.

"What's that?"

"Remake *Mimming*. I have the hilt, if only I had what was left of the blade!"

Hildegund gave a light laugh and left the room to get something. Moments later she came back with a small wooden casket. "Here you are," she said, "I couldn't bear to leave that famous blade in pieces for any passing peasant to find and make into a kitchen knife, so I gathered up the shards and put them in this box. What will you do with them?"

"Ah! If only I could take them back to Weland to reforge them!"

"Weland is just a legend."

"A master smith of old, then."

"What about a master smith of today – Brom, for instance?"

Waldere sighed, "He's only a local blacksmith."

"But he makes swords for the king!"

"True. I will ask him what can be done."

He found Brom sweating at his forge, hammering a bar of cherry red iron. Brom stopped his work as soon as he recognized the great man and asked how he could help. Waldere displayed the fragments of *Mimming*. "Can you do anything with this?" he said.

"Is that *Mimming*? How did it break? No, there's no need to tell me. I know the lay. How does it go: '*Weland's work will never weaken!*' Ha! But it did. It shattered on Hagen's helmet."

"That's right."

Brom examined one of the shards. "Poor quality steel – brittle."

"But..."

"I know: its an 'heirloom sword worked by Weland'. But Weland is a story. These old swords are all very well to hang on a wall, but no good for fighting – they couldn't get the steel in those days. Now, that other sword you had..."

"The urepos."

"That performed well if the lay is true. May I see it?"

Waldere sent a retainer to bring it, and while they waited Brom told him about the way the best old swords were made using a technique called pattern welding, with tough and flexible steel in the middle of the blade, and a strip of hard steel welded around the edges.

When the urepos was brought in he examined it carefully, and showed Waldere a swirling grainy pattern in the metal. "This pattern shows that it is finest Damascus steel. Now, watch this." He put the blade on the anvil, then put his foot on it and proceeded to bend the blade until it was bent to about 45 degrees. Then he let go of it and it sprang back into shape. "Most other blades would break if they were too brittle, or stay bent if they were too soft. This Damascus steel is just right."

Waldere understood then how that blade, light as it was, had performed so well during his time of need.

"I can remake *Mimming* by hammering these fragments together with rods of Damascus steel, and then you will say: *'Brom's work will never weaken!'* Yes, that's it! Never mind Weland. Put me in a saga!"

And that's how that fabled blade, *Mimming*, came to be reforged, and came to be more fabulous than ever.

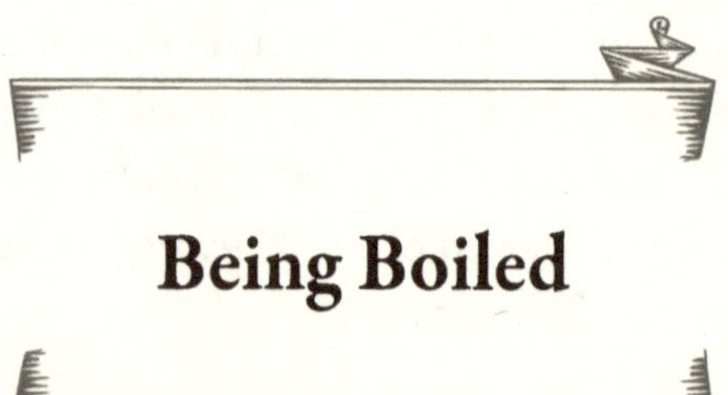

Being Boiled

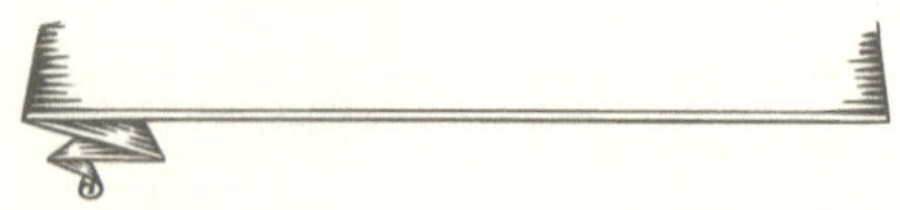

It was a gruelling journey for Malrede and his five retainers, though fortunately the weather was dry for late Autumn. Their long detour around Burgundia meant that they avoided the highest regions of the alps. Travelling through Gallia was safe enough for a party of fully armed men, as the *Pax Romana* still held to some extent in that region. It was different when they got to the border of the Ostrogoth kingdom. Of course, Malrede and his men spoke the same language, Gothic, and the sense of kinship between Ostrogoth and Visigoth was still strong, but to avoid future problems, and to make sure of their way, Malrede hired a local guide.

When they arrived in Etseliri they were treated with suspicion at first, but when Attila had assured himself that they were who they said they were, he welcomed them with open arms and lavish hospitality. Malrede was invited to join him at the high table, and his retainers were given places of honour among his own retainers.

The difficult journey had been good for Malrede as it had toughened him physically. Though still slight of frame, he was no longer the effete counsellor. He had gained muscle, his features were somewhat weather-beaten, and his clothes were the worse for wear – and just as well, for Attila respected physical toughness above anything else. Nevertheless, Malrede had no illusions about himself. He was proud of his adventure, even though it had failed – proud of the way he had struggled on and found his way to Attila's court. But he knew that his future success lay in diplomacy and not in strength of arms. He had information that was valuable to Attila, and he was determined to make the most of it.

Attila, for his part, was eager to find out everything he could about Waldere. He had heard something of the battle of the Vosges, but Waldere's prowess in that battle only made him all the more eager to get him back – whether for promotion or punishment, he had not decided. He was angered to learn that Gunther had betrayed him by going over to Waldere and forming an alliance with him. "If I ever get my hands on him, I'll...well, you'll see tomorrow. In the meantime, tell me about Ælfhere's forces and anything you know about his intentions."

"My lord, his army is no bigger than when he agreed to the treaty. As for his intentions, I have no idea what they are now. As I have told you, I managed to persuade him to send Waldere back – but he outsmarted me."

Attila gave a hearty laugh. "He would have outsmarted better men than you!" Then his laugh became a growl. "I want him back at any cost!"

Malrede sensed an opportunity. "My lord, there is a way..."

"Don't tell me to invest Burdigala again! It is a long, hard march from here to Aquitania, and it is late in the season!"

"No. Demand the return of Hildegund, and when Hereric refuses – which he will, because she is with Waldere – lay waste the whole of Burgundia. When Ælfhere sees that, he will have no choice but to send Waldere to you."

Attila chuckled at a private thought. "That may not be necessary. Something has come up which will make an attack on Burgundia seem like a side show."

He said no more, and Malrede was diplomat enough not to ask.

Next evening, Malrede was intrigued to note a huge cauldron in front of the high table. A slave was feeding wood to the fire beneath it and it was coming to the boil. Malrede wondered what tasty delicacy Attila was preparing. He also noticed that there were only men present in the hall.

"I am impressed with your command of our language," said Attila.

"I have been learning it ever since Waldere became your hostage, as I knew it would come in handy one day."

"How's your Latin?"

"It is like another mother tongue to me."

"Read this then."

Attila handed him a letter written in the careful script of a Roman scribe. Malrede perused it quickly, and, despite the diplomat in him, couldn't help revealing surprise at its contents: "It is from Honoria, the sister of the emperor Valentinian. She says that she has been betrothed against her will to the former consul Herculanus, and asks for your help to escape the engagement."

"She enclosed this with it." Attila showed him a gold ring. "How do you interpret that?"

Malrede could tell by the intense look in Attila's eyes that this was a make or break question. Attila was looking for an astute answer, and if he got it right, his fortune would be made – on the other hand...

Just then, cries of protest interrupted their conversation. A prisoner was being led in by four guards. They tied a rope to the chain round his body, threw the other end over one of the rafters and hauled him into the air. A moment later, he was suspended over the cauldron, which was now at boiling point.

"I am not a cruel man," said Attila, "but this man tried to kill me."

The guards lowered the man into the boiling water up to the knees. He screamed and kicked and begged for mercy.

"Names!" barked one of the guards.

"I told you!"

"There's more! Keep talking."

"I will. Take me out!"

They hauled him clear of the water.

"Ellac."

"We have him already."

"Banda."

"He's fled."

Attila gave a sign, and the man was lowered into the cauldron again, this time up to the thighs.

"Balamber! Balamber! Balamber!"

Suddenly, a man at the back of the hall sprang to his feet and tried to run from the room. He was stopped by the guards at the door and arrested.

"I thought so," said Attila. "That will do."

Malrede thought for a moment that that signalled the end of the torture. It did, but in the most horrific way. At a nod from Attila, the rope was cut and the man was dropped into the boiling cauldron. His screams were terrible, and many of Attila's nobles were white-faced as they listened.

"We boil lobsters alive, don't we?" said Attila, nonchalantly, "and they've done nothing wrong. This man deserved it. Also, look at the faces of my lords. It is a lesson that they won't forget – you too perhaps. Now, what were you saying?"

Attila turned back to the letter as though the boiling alive of his would-be assassin was no more important than the lobsters that were being served at that very moment (a touch of black humour on the part of the great man, or just a coincidence?)

Unsettling though the incident had been, it had given Malrede time to think. He believed that he had read Attila's mind and knew what he wanted him to say: "By itself, the letter is a plea for help. Perhaps she wants you to threaten Valentinian with an attack on Ravenna – but with the ring, it is an offer of her hand in marriage."

Attila gave a broad grin, and Malrede knew he had got it right. "That is how I interpret it. Now, what do you think would be a suitable dowry for the sister of the emperor?"

Malrede's mind raced. He remembered his previous advice to Attila and his reply, and built on that: "The kingdom of Burgundia?"

"It's a start – but remember, she is the sister of the emperor."

"All of Gallia to its former boundaries."

Attila gave a satisfied laugh. "What do you say to half the western Empire? After all, I have most of it already!"

The diplomat in Malrede thought that Attila was overplaying his hand. Even if Valentinian agreed to the marriage, he would never agree to such an enormous dowry – but he had to be careful what he said, "Perhaps, my lord."

"It would take a master diplomat to negotiate it," said Attila.

A genius, thought Malrede.

"And I think you are the man."

Malrede was shocked to the core. Had Attila no diplomats of his own? How could he entrust him with such a task after only knowing him for one day? But then, he had made Waldere ordwyga, even though he was a Visigoth. Attila was a judge of character, and Malrede was not without a sense of pride that he had recognized his diplomatic abilities – on the other hand, it was mission impossible. It could only end in failure and what then?

"If you succeed you will be richly rewarded. I will give you a hall, retainers, land – and Hildaz, the most beautiful woman in Pannonia; and you can help yourself from my treasury," Attila paused, as though marvelling at his own generosity, then added, "But if you fail..."

Malrede couldn't help looking at the cauldron, where the dead body of the assassin, now boiled to a horrible pink colour, lay suspended in the water. Attila gave a raucous laugh. "I told you I am not a cruel man! Being boiled is for those who betray me! No. You will get the opposite of what I promised. Instead of being raised to the highest, you will be thrown among the lowest – a kitchen thrall – that will be your place. You can scour bronze pots with bunches of chain. But that will not be necessary, for I trust you to succeed. I will send you with 20 retainers. You can take your five Visigoths and another 15 of mine to make sure that, if you do fail, you don't flee to Burdigala."

"My lord," said Malrede quickly, "that I will never do; a worse punishment awaits me there!"

"Do you accept the mission?"

Malrede wanted to say, What choice have I? but the diplomat in him urged him to choose his words carefully. However, there was something he had to say, whatever the consequences: "My lord, if I am to bring about success, I need to negotiate on more reasonable terms..."

"Are you saying I am unreasonable?" said Attila with a frown.

It was a dangerous moment, but the diplomat found a form of words to finesse it: "No, but Valentinian might think so. From his point of view he might be glad to secure such a powerful ally through marriage, but what is the point of a powerful ally if he loses half his empire. Let me advise you again; ask for Gallia only."

"But I want Hispania as well. He can keep North Africa. It's mostly desert anyway."

"Valentinian might reply that Hispania is not his to give. It belongs to the Visigoths now."

Attila was laughing again. "Ha! I see I was right in my choice! You see all the twists and turns like a weasel in a burrow!"

"Of course, the counter-argument is that they are foederati and still under the control of Rome."

"Better and better!"

"So will you take my advice?"

"No. Half the Empire or nothing."

Malrede wanted to continue arguing, but he knew that Attila's word was final, and he didn't want to be next in the cauldron. Nor did he want to be a kitchen thrall. He would do his best, of course, but you didn't need to be a master diplomat to know that Valentinian would baulk at the dowry. The only thing he could think of was to negotiate for Gallia in the hope that Attila would accept it after all.

Mission Impossible

The journey was hard. It was late in the year, though the Alpine passes were still open. Their guide led them along winding ways, ever ascending, with abrupt precipices below, and snow-topped mountains above. When the way was particularly steep, they alighted from their horses and walked, giving them a better opportunity to appreciate the long vista of mountains where immense glaciers exhibited their frozen horrors. The deep silence of these solitudes was a stimulant to meditation, and Malrede often found himself thinking about his mission. In one sense he was very proud of what he had achieved. Not so long ago he had been a counsellor in a kingdom in a corner of former Gallia, and now he was on a mission to the emperor himself on behalf of the most powerful man in the world. On the other hand the chances that his mission would succeed were miniscule, and the consequences of failure were unthinkable.

His thoughts were broken only by the scream of vultures seen towering round some cliff below, or by the cry of the eagle sailing high in the air. Those soaring eagles inspired him to dream of success: of fabulous riches, land, retainers, the delectable Hildaz, but the croak of the vultures dragged him down to visions of himself in a ragged apron scouring huge bronze cooking pots with chains.

After traversing these regions for many miles, they began to descend towards Intercisa and the going became easier. From Intercisa it was an easy journey along the Via Flaminia to Ravenna. And then – civilization! Of course, Malrede had seen a shadow of it in Burdigala, but in a decrepit state: the amphitheatre was half gone, its fine, dressed stone blocks raided for other uses, and the interior used as a rubbish dump. The aqueduct was broken in several places, and had not delivered water for as long as he could remember. The baths had fallen into disuse, and the building was used as a grain store. The governor's palace was maintained as King Ælfhere's royal residence, but the Visigoth craftsmen had neither the skill nor the materials to match old Roman work, and it had been patched up with roughly-coursed rubble and wood painted to look like marble. But here, everything was in good repair. The aqueduct, which could be seen from the road, was magnificent; two tiers of soaring arches which seemed to go on for mile after mile. Ravenna itself was even more magnificent. The gatehouse was a huge building, with two tiers of arched windows either side of an enormous central arched gateway, with not a stone or a tile missing – so different from the dilapidated defences of Burdigala.

Malrede presented his credentials to the captain of the guard; Attila's seal, Honoria's ring and letter, and explained his mission, and an armed escort was arranged. He was led past one enormous public building after another, but the imperial palace was a sight to take the breath away. It was built around a large peristyle courtyard which was surrounded by many elaborate rooms of great height. It seemed as though there were people everywhere, but most of them were statues in various poses, painted to look real. Malrede and his retainers were shown to one of the buildings and given refreshments, after which he was escorted, with just two of his men, to the Aula Regia, an enormous rectangular hall used as an audience chamber. It was impressive beyond words. Corinthian columns rose to an impossibly high vaulted ceiling, and a huge semi-circular window, glazed with triangular panes of glass, lit it with the brilliance of a summer day. A series of mosaic portraits were ranged along the walls, and at the far end was a huge mosaic of the imperial eagle, symbolising the might of the emperors of Rome.

He was shown to an apse in the south wall where a diplomat was awaiting him.

"*Salve*. May I request an audience with the emperor?" said Malrede in his politest Latin.

"Salve, and welcome to Ravenna," said the diplomat. "My name is Priscius. I will hear your petition, and if I judge it necessary, I will arrange an audience."

"I have been sent by Attila," said Malrede.

Priscius already knew this, but bowed slightly to acknowledge the importance of such a mission. "I was once an envoy to Attila, so I may be able to help you. Show me your credentials and then explain what it is about."

Malrede showed him Attila's seal and Honoria's letter and ring, then explained Attila's terms. Priscius frowned and shook his head. "We know all about this. Honoria acted foolishly to get out of a marriage that her brother, the emperor, arranged for her, but Attila has misinterpreted the letter. No offer of marriage was intended. Indeed, it was an act of treason to send that letter, and Honoria has been imprisoned."

All of Malrede's carefully prepared negotiating tactics were negated at a stroke by those words. Instead, he had to fall back on the threats that Attila had made: "Attila believes this ring is a token of engagement, and he will take Honoria by force if necessary."

Priscius gave a faint smile. "I have heard that three of his subject kingdoms have rebelled against him. He had better put his own house in order before he comes after ours."

Malrede could think of nothing more to say except, "Then you had better prepare for war."

"Believe me," said Priscius with a note of complacency, "we have already started. Even now our magister militum, Aetius, is building an alliance that will send Attila back to Hungvar with his tail between his legs."

Malrede was about to say something more, but Priscius raised his hand to stop him. "We thank you for your embassy. The audience is over."

The guards stamped their feet and rapped the butts of their spears on the floor to signal that Malrede and his attendants should leave, but already, with that first step out of the apse, Malrede's quick mind was working out what he should do next.

A plan was formed before he even got back to his retainers: "Our embassy has failed," he announced, "for now. But I intend to try again when the emperor has had time to reconsider." He had no intention of trying again because he knew it would be futile, but he needed an excuse to linger in Ravenna. "In the meantime, you are free to enjoy yourselves – as long as you make no trouble. Ravenna has *balneae*, *tabernae* and *lupinaria* in plenty..."

"What?" said one of the Huns.

"Baths, bars and brothels."

"Come on, lads, what are we waiting for?" said a Visigoth, and they were away.

I'll give them until tomorrow night, thought Malrede. And sure enough, by the following evening, not one of his retainers was to be seen, even those who had been given strict orders by Attila not to let him out of their sight, so it was easy enough to get away. He prepared himself by buying a Roman tunic and having his hair cut short, Roman style. His plan was to escape to Rome, disguised as a Roman, and to lose himself in that great city. Of course, he would avoid the Via Flaminia and travel by an indirect route.

It was a good plan – except for one little mistake. Malrede rejoined the Via Flaminia about a mile north of Rome so that he could enter the city by the Porto Flaminia. He was nearing the gates, when suddenly someone shouted in the Hunnic language: "There he is!" and moments later he was on the pavement, gagged and bound. Attila's retainers had missed him and had guessed that he would head for Rome. They failed to catch up with him on the Via Flaminia, and so had lain in wait at the gate for a few days. Luckily for them, their guess had proved right, otherwise Attila would have had something to say about it.

In the event, it was Malrede who got the hard word. To have failed was bad enough, but to have attempted to flee was inexcusable. His punishment, therefore, would be somewhat harsher than the kitchen – and that was how he ended up being dragged in chains to the boiling cauldron. There was nothing he could do, so he resolved to die with dignity. He would avoid any attempt to plead with Attila, and would not scream when he was lowered into the boiling water – but when that water hissed around him he let out a howl that would have melted the heart of the Devil himself, though Attila seemed to find it amusing.

Nobody mourned his passing, except perhaps, just a little, Hildaz. That was the third promising young man she'd been robbed of, and she was very much afraid that her blossoming womanhood would go to waste.

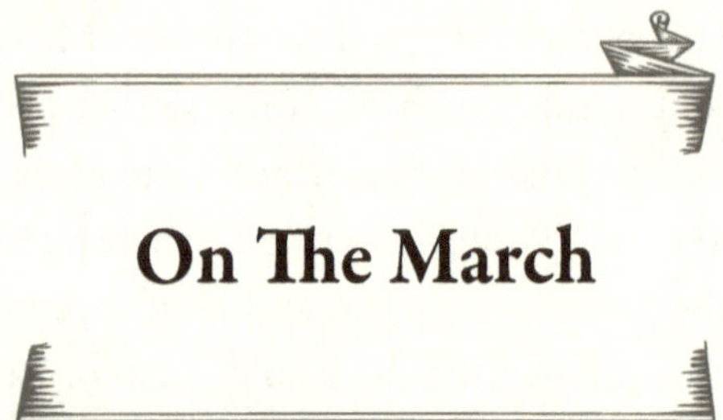

On The March

Attila now declared that he would take up arms on behalf of his promised bride, and, bearing in mind the advice of his recently boiled diplomat, planned to make Burgundia his first target. So as soon as the campaigning season began, he crossed the River Rhine at Confluentes and confronted King Hereric, who had marched out to meet him. Hereric had sent for help to Aetius, Ælfhere and other members of the alliance, but Aetius was not ready, and Ælfhere could not get to Burgundia soon enough. Hereric's army, though one of the largest of the post-Roman kingdoms, was a mere speck compared to Attila's hordes, and was soon wiped out.

Attila then divided his army into two parts; a smaller part which marched northwards to subdue Francia, and the main part which marched westward to subdue Aquitania and Hispania, called Regnum Gothorum by the Visigoths. His first objective was Aurelianum, as, from there, he could dominate the whole south west. But the city was strongly fortified and managed to hold out.

This gave Aetius time to assemble his field army. It was the strangest patchwork of fighting forces ever assembled by a Roman general, consisting of Roman legions, auxiliaries, foederati and allies including: Francii, Sarmatae, Liticiani, Saxones, Riparii, and what was left of the Burgundians. He sent word to Theodoric and Ælfhere to march north and join him at Aurelianum, where he hoped to catch Attila at a disadvantage.

When Ælfhere received the message, he delegated the responsibility to Waldere, being too old and feeble to lead his army himself. He also sent Eawa to Armorica to request that Aurelius join them with his *I Britannicus* at Genabum. From there they would march towards Aurelianum where they would join forces with Aetius.

Eawa did not waste time refreshing himself after his journey. He hurried into the audience chamber and barged to the front of a queue of supplicants pleading, in a loud voice, "Affairs of state!"

Uther recognized him at once, and there was no need to ask the reason for his brusque intrusion. "The call has come," he said to Aurelius, and Aurelius said to Eawa, "We are ready. We will march at dawn. Meanwhile, for heaven's sake, take some refreshment! You look done in!"

Aurelius had said that his legion was ready, and it was in the sense that it was ready to march. But it had never marched before, let alone fought a battle, and one thing after another seemed to go wrong before they finally made a start. The problem was that not enough thought had been given to logistics. Uther had been successful in expanding his legion, which now, with its auxiliaries, numbered over 3,000 men, but he had failed to provide enough packhorses and wagons, which had to be commandeered at the last minute, causing inevitable delay. But at last, in the late afternoon, they were able to march.

Eawa seemed much interested in the legion, which he was seeing in full array for the first time. "Your men are well equipped," he commented. "Only our professional army have arms and armour. The levies fight with whatever they have."

"You are looking at my elite bodyguard," said Aurelius. "Let us wait here for a while and see the rank and file as they march past."

Eawa and Uther guided their horses to the side of the road, while Uther stayed at the head of the column. One by one the cohorts passed by, but Eawa did not change his opinion. "Their arms are simple enough, I see. A sword, a javelin, a shield and a leather cap – but you should see the dregs of Ælfhere's army! Waldere sent out a call to all men of military age. Not everybody turned up, but those that did were a sorry lot, and there was not enough time to train or equip them."

"Not one of my men has any experience of battle," said Aurelius with a note of anxiety. "I'm afraid they will run at the first sight of blood!"

Not that they appeared afraid just then. They marched with a confident step to the sound of their own singing. After all, this was what they had been training for years – it mattered little that they were marching in the opposite direction to Britannia, the important thing was that they were going to show the enemy what they could do. Despite his doubts, Aurelius' heart lifted as they marched past. The arms and armour of the rank and file were, indeed, basic, but he had felt it important for morale that they looked the part, and accordingly he had equipped each man with a standard grey tunic and a large oval shield which bore the emblem of the Red Dragon of Britannia.

The first part of their march was through Armorican territory, and the spirits of the soldiers were lifted further by the cheers of the people in the towns and villages through which they passed. Those people understood little enough of the complex politics that had brought the legion in that direction, but they were all too familiar with the horror stories told about Attila and his hordes. Often that name was shouted from their midst: "Save us from Attila!"

"They seem terrified," remarked Aurelius.

"They have good reason," replied Eawa. "Attila has a terrible reputation. If a town refuses to surrender, he executes all the men, enslaves the women, and razes it to the ground. On the other hand, if a town surrenders, he can be magnanimous. The fist and the glove – it's a powerful tactic."

"What is he like in battle?" said Aurelius thoughtfully. "I mean, what kind of tactics does he use?"

"The Huns are horse archers. They ride at tremendous speed and use their bows as they ride."

Aurelius frowned. "We have few cavalry. Surely, they will ride us down!"

"If your infantry stand firm, they have nothing to fear. The idea is for your infantry to hold the line while your archers shoot at the horses."

Aurelius brightened. "Our archers are our great strength."

Eawa nodded. "Yes, I have heard of the prowess of Armorican archers. They will be most welcome. Each part of Aetius' coalition will do what it does best."

"I have heard that Attila is invincible," said Aurelius doubtfully. "Where does that idea come from?"

"It seems that everything predicts it: Roman legends as well as theirs."

"What do you mean?"

"Rome's twelve centuries were augured by twelve vultures, which appeared to Romulus when Rome was founded. This is the twelfth century! And then, there is the way in which he killed his brother for the kingship of Hungvar. It is said that it is a parallel to the fratricide of Remus, the harbinger of a new cycle of worldly power...and then – there is the sword..."

Aurelius felt an electrifying tingle in his spine. "The sword?" he said, as memories of Merlin and the Sword of Albion flickered through his mind.

"It is said that he found the Sword of Tengri – Tengri is their war god. Their legends tell that the wielder of the Sword of Tengri will be ruler of the whole world. That legend united the tribes behind him and makes them believe they are invincible in battle."

At that moment, something changed for Aurelius. Until then he had seen the Sword of Albion as a wizard's fantasy, and had never quite believed in it. His scholarly mind had rejected it just as completely as Uther's practical mind. It was only Merlin's absolute conviction about the importance of the Sword that had carried him along – but now, he could see for himself the power of a symbol. If Attila could conquer half the world with the Sword of Tengri, he could reconquer Britannia with the Sword of Albion – yes, there were a few problems in his way. First he had to survive the impending battle, and secondly he had to find his own symbolic sword, but the idea gave him renewed heart.

At the end of the third day's march, Aurelius' scouts said that they had sighted a huge camp, which, judging by its regular disposition, was clearly a Roman camp. "Aetius," said Eawa, confirming Aurelius' expectations with a single word.

It was not long before Aurelius and Uther found themselves inside Aetius' tent being introduced to the great man himself. He was tall, and slightly balding, and his lined features indicating his age. Avitus had told them that he was 60, but his stance was perfectly erect and filled with nervous energy, and his face had an intense look that radiated charisma. "You are welcome," he said, gripping his forearm with customary Roman greeting. "We have need of every man, and a well-trained legion is beyond price."

Aurelius tried to say something, but found himself speechless in front of the man who had defended the Empire against the barbarians for a generation, and who had singlehandedly put together this unlikely coalition against Attila – Rome's last army. He felt unworthy – like a schoolboy playing at war, who suddenly bumps into a real soldier. When he found his voice at last, he tried to mumble an apology for his legion. Phrases like "not well-trained at all" and "not enough men by far," were all that were identifiable in the incoherent mumble. Aetius laughed and slapped him on the shoulder to reassure him. "I have heard reports of the *I Britannicus*, and believe me, they will do well enough! It is the Alans who concern me most – not because they are not good fighting men, but because their loyalty is, shall we say, uncertain."

Uther, who had been bullish about the *I Britannicus* to the point of over-confidence, had been overawed at the sight of Aetius' camp, which contained row upon row of leather tents in orderly formations which seemed to stretch for miles. Eawa had told him that the Roman contingent, though mainly auxiliaries, numbered around 15,000. For the first time he began to understand his brother's anxiety about the small size of their army.

Aetius continued to express his appreciation and emphasised that there was more to an army than numbers. "Untrained men are worse than useless. They get in the way, and when the heat is on, they run away."

The great man had succeeded in putting the Aurelius and Uther at ease, and what is more, had inspired their loyalty. Despite the problems he faced – and there were many – he seemed calmly confident. That confidence was infectious. Aurelius, who, half an hour ago, had feared that his tiny, untrained army would be wiped out, now felt a surge of enthusiasm for their cause.

Just then, another man came into the tent, and exchanged a few words with Aetius in the Gothic language. He was dressed in an odd mixture of Germanic and Hunnic war-gear, and his right hand was missing.

"This is Waldere," said Aetius, "from the independent Visigothic kingdom which we used call Aquitania Secunda. I think you may have heard of him in the Latin version of his name, Waltharius."

"Waltharius! Surely not the Victor of the Vosges!"

"Is that what they call me?" said Waldere in a tone of self-deprecation.

"And the hero of a lay which we call *Waltharius Manu Fortis* in Latin."

"It's not *manu fortis* now," said Waldere, holding up his stump. "But I still hope to serve Aetius. I have a score to settle with Attila! And *this* will help me!" with these words he touched his gold-wound sword hilt with his left hand.

"Is that the famous *Mimming*?"

"Yes, the work of Weland, reforged by Brom."

Brom would have been proud to have heard his name mentioned in the same breath as the legendary smith.

"I am not so good with my left hand as I was with my right, but I will use this sword to inspire my men," Waldere continued.

Once again, Aurelius had cause to reflect on the power of a sword as a symbol.

Aetius went on to explain how he would deploy Waldere and his army: "Waltharius has brought 2,000 men and will fight alongside Theodoric's Visigoths, as they are part of the same people, and understand each other's language and way of fighting. It is a most valuable addition to my forces."

Waldere gave a slight bow to acknowledge the compliment, but Aetius had not finished, and went on to elaborate on the value of the man himself. "But Waldere is much more than a master of martial arts, he is an expert in the Hunnic style of fighting: he used to be Attila's *magister militum*."

"I wouldn't call it that," said Waldere. "*War chief* would be more accurate."

"Whatever you call it, he knows all there is to know about their weapons, horses and tactics, and that knowledge is a pearl of price in helping me to plan my deployments."

"What is the latest news about Attila?" said Aurelius.

"You'll have heard that he defeated King Hereric and laid waste to Burgundia after crossing River Rhine. Next was Augustobonum,[11] but it appears that it was saved by a charismatic bishop by the name of Lupus – though I find that hard to believe! It is said that, when the magister militum and his men were cowering behind the city walls, he went to meet Attila dressed in full bishop's regalia. He is reported to have said: 'You are *Flagelum Dei* – the Scourge of God – but we in Augustobonum are penitent. Spare us and unleash His vengeance on sinners who will not repent.' It seems that Attila liked his new cognomen so well that he spared the city from destruction and marched on to Aurelianum. Another branch of his army was sent to attack Francia, but King Gunther held out, and now Attila is in retreat."

"Retreat?"

"Ha! That's a misleading word. My guess is that it is a strategic withdrawal to find a place where his horse archers can be used to best advantage. He will choose the Campi Catalaunici,[12] I think. Tomorrow, we will pursue him."

"But we have just arrived!" protested Aurelius.

"And just in time!" said Aetius. "I'm afraid your legion will have little rest. You should inform your tribunes. Then rest yourself a while. I will send for you later for the council of war."

Aurelius and Uther went to see how their legion was settling down. They had been allocated a square space at the far end of the camp, and were proceeding to put up their leather tents in the same pattern as the Romans. Aurelius called his tribunes to his tent, and told them the news. In particular, that they must be ready to march the following day, then he left Uther to sort out the 1001 petty problems of logistics –

a wagon had broken down, sixteen tents were missing, the equites did not know where to stable their horses, and so on.

It was not long before Aetius' summons came. He suggested that only Aurelius come to the meeting, as his tent was already overcrowded with allied leaders. That suited Aurelius. He needed Uther's bullish temperament to sort out the logistical problems, and not to get into arguments with Aetius over trivialities.

He was on his way there when a great disturbance at the entrance to the camp announced the arrival of another army – and there was Gunther, sitting awkwardly on a special saddle made to support his wooden leg, and beside him, Hagen, looking fierce with his eyeless socket and scarred cheek beneath his boar-crested helmet.

"Just in time!" said Waldere.

"It's a long way from Francia!" said Gunther.

"It's good to see you again, Gunther, and you too, Hagen," said Waldere. "But I can't linger. Aetius has summoned me to a meeting. You should come too, Gunther, if you are able."

"My arse hurts more than my leg on this damn saddle!" protested Gunther. "I'll send Hagen instead."

Hagen dismounted, glad to be of service, and walked towards Aetius' tent with Waldere. As they walked, Hagen noticed the familiar gold-bound hilt. "Is that *Mimming*?" he said.

"Yes," said Waldere, half drawing it. "Ælfhere's blacksmith, a man called Brom, reforged it for me."

"I wish somebody could reforge my eye!"

"Or my right hand! I'm not the warrior I was!"

"Never mind. Our job is to lead, it is up to others to do the fighting."

The two friends entered Aetius' tent together, and found Aetius and his lords in the middle of a heated discussion which seemed to be taking place in several languages at once. At last, Aetius called them to order, and they sat down around a long table on which a large map had been spread out. Aetius addressed them in Latin, with an occasional remark in Gothic. His father had been a Goth, and this fact, and his fluency in the language, had gone a long way in winning over the Visigoths and the other Germanic tribes.

"Tomorrow at first light we begin our march against Attila..." he began. He was interrupted by grunts of enthusiasm from around the table. "...I am convinced that he will make a stand at the Campi Catalaunici... here," said Aetius, jabbing at the map with a long, bony finger.

Just then, he noticed Hagen, and Waldere introduced him. "My lord, this is Hagen. King Gunther is here, but his leg is troubling him after the long journey. Hagen is his magister militum."

"Welcome, Hagano," said Aetius. "You bring another valuable addition to our forces, the deployment of which I am just about to explain." He bent over the map and continued: "I will take the left flank with the Romans and you, Theodoric, Waltharius and Hagano, will take the right. Sangiban's Alans, and Aurelius' Armoricans will hold the centre. I want the Armorican archers at the front."

Sangiban was immediately on his feet. "The centre! My lord, you know too well that many of my men say that we should not be fighting alongside Romans, a former enemy – is this how you punish us?"

Aurelius, too, felt that he should speak up. "My lord, my army is as yet untried. If you put them at the heart of the battle, they will surely break!"

Suddenly everyone was talking at once, disagreeing with Aetius' dispositions for their own reasons. Aetius let them rant for a while, then raised his hand for silence.

"My lords," he said with calm confidence. "You know how the Huns fight. They are horse archers, not infantry. They encircle their enemies' flanks and strike hard from the side, or behind. All the centre needs to do is to hold fast! We, on the flanks will bear the brunt of the battle!"

A powerfully-built Goth rose to his feet. He was an impressive sight, with long blonde hair, streaked with grey. His lined face and grizzled locks showed that he was well into his fifties. He spoke in rough Latin with the belligerence customary among the Germanic tribes, who believed that it is good luck to boast before a battle: "Never mind 'bear the brunt'!" he growled, "I will take the battle to Attila!"

Aurelius guessed that this must be the legendary Theodoric who had led the Gothic settlement of Hispania and was now Aetius' principal ally.

"As long as you wait for the right moment," said Aetius, who clearly mistrusted his ally's martial enthusiasm. "Whatever you do, don't leave the centre exposed."

Sangiban sprang up again. "That's what will happen! You can't trust the Visigoths!"

Theodoric reached for his sword hilt, but Aetius, who was close by, clapped his hand over Theodoric's hand. "My lords!" he said, through gritted teeth. "We are allies, are we not? We will fight as one. Theodoric, you will hold the left flank until the enemy retreats."

As he said these words, he gave Theodoric a steely glance, and Theodoric gave way to it. What hold over him Aetius had, Aurelius could not imagine, but it was enough.

"...but, mark me, when the time comes, I will take the fight to Attila!" roared Theodoric.

"And I will be right behind you!" cried Waldere, fired up by Theodoric's zeal. "I have an old score to settle!" and he held up his severed right wrist as a sign of it.

Later, Eawa told Aurelius more about the Germanic custom of boasting before a battle. A boast had to be fulfilled, or the boaster was dishonoured, so it was their way of working themselves up to do great deeds, personal honour in battle being their main aim. It meant that they were brave beyond the call of duty, but sometimes foolhardy.

Aetius said a private word to Waldere, then asked him to speak to the allies, introducing him as follows: "You will have heard of Waltharius from the lay, and you will know that he is a master of the martial arts – but he is more that that to us. He was once Attila's *ordwyga* – war chief – and he can give us valuable advice about the way the Huns fight, and the way to fight back."

There was much that Waldere could have told them about Hunnic tactics, but not much that would have been much use to a mixed group of allies with their own traditions of fighting, and no time to practice any manouvres he might recommend, so he picked out a few important points.

"Above all," he said, "hold the line. The Huns will try to confuse you. They will charge at you with lightning speed, shoot their bows and gallop away again. Whatever you do, don't charge after them, because others are waiting to outflank you. Hold the line, overlap your shields, and there is little they can do."

"But how can we fight back!" urged Theodoric.

First, archers, then javelins, then, if you know how, use the tactic called 'Dragon's Mouth', which the Romans call 'Forceps': when the Huns attack, open the shieldwall, let in 30 or so men, then close the shieldwall again, while others behind the shieldwall finish them off. It is a difficult manouvre, and should only be attempted by those who have practiced it."

"My men can do that," said Theodoric.

"What of those who can't?" said Sangiban.

"Remember my most important piece of advice: hold the line, hold the line, hold the line! Eventually the Huns will run out of arrows or tire, then you can charge them, on foot in the centre, cavalry on the flanks. But wait for the signal, wait for the signal, wait for the signal! If you charge too soon they will mow you down like wheat."

"Anything else?" said Aetius.

"Plenty, but that's all we can use without time to practice."

"Very well, let us go over the plan again," said Aetius and he went on to repeat the main points, demonstrating the positions and movements on the map. Finally, he said, "And remember Waltharius' words: hold the line!"

He closed the meeting by thanking them all for attending and dismissing them with the words: "Tomorrow we will send Attila back to Pannonia with his tail between his legs!"

"Or to Valhalla!" added Sangiban.

"Hell, more like," said Theodoric.

"A man like that is worthy of Valhalla, even though he is our enemy," said Sangiban as they left the tent, and they could be heard arguing, though more agreeably than before, as they made their way to their camp.

"Stay a moment, Aurelius," said Aetius as Aurelius was about to leave. Aurelius turned round and came back to the table.

"Theodoric will spend half the night boasting and feasting, and the other half in a sound sleep – the sleep of the dead drunk – while I will lay awake, worrying."

Aurelius was surprised. "After all the battles you have fought!"

Aetius laughed. "Oh, it is not death I am afraid of! That will come soon enough. I am not like the young legionary who lies awake calculating his chances – dead, wounded, or alive and in one piece! No, it is Rome I worry about. If Attila wins this battle, the Empire that I have spend my whole life defending is finished."

Aurelius, who had been inspired by Aetius' confidence at the council, and by the large number of the allied commanders, was suddenly doubtful. "I thought that with such a large coalition...I mean..."

Aetius looked at him squarely. "You want to ask me what our chances are? I will be honest with you. In fact, that is why I asked you to stay. You are the only other commander who is Roman..."

Aurelius was about to say something, but Aetius waved it away and continued. "Yes, I know, Romano-British. You have mixed parentage, but so have I. My father was a Goth. That's why I can speak their language. You, like me are *dux et patricius*[13] – well, rather more, *dux et rex*.[14] What I am trying to say is that we both have had the advantage of a Roman education, so you are the only one of the allied commanders to whom I can express my doubts without fear of misunderstanding."

"Doubts?"

"Yes. Give me the three legions I commanded in Gallia, and I would wipe Attila off the face of the earth, but what have I? Hardly any regular legionaries – just my personal bodyguard. The rest of my legion is made up of auxiliaries of varying quality. Your *I Britannicus* is better!"

Aurelius shook his head. "There are not enough of them, they are ill-equipped, lacking in experience..."

"But Roman...yes, I know, Romano-British. It doesn't matter what you call them. They are citizens fighting for their country, and that is everything. Rome achieved its greatness when its legions were manned by citizens. Anyone else will always have divided loyalties..."

"Surely Rome still has citizens – where are they now?"

"Living dissipated lives: the arena, banqueting, boozing, fornicating, or cheering on chariots or gladiators, or gambling, or amassing gold. They've forgotten the Sack of Rome – it was a generation ago – but it will be sacked again if we don't beat Attila! – and they don't seem to care. They prefer to pay others to fight in their place..."

"So you hire mercenaries..."

"Not mercenaries exactly – foederati. Tribes with a treaty obligation to fight for Rome – but their loyalty is just as questionable!"

"What about your allies?"

"You have seen the squabbling! The irony is that Attila is doing me a service by binding them together. They all know that if Attila is not defeated their petty kingdoms will be swept away."

Aurelius grimaced and Aetius read his thoughts. "Yes, and Armorica too. Even Britannia would not be safe."

Aurelius was thoughtful. An idea had come to him, but he hardly dared express it. At last, he found the courage. "If we win this battle, will you help me to retake Britannia?"

Aetius shrugged. "That is not the first time I have been asked to help Britannia. A long time ago I was sent a message: The barbarians drive us to the sea, the sea drives us to the barbarians; between these two means of death, we are either killed or drowned... or words to that effect, and my reply then was the same as it is now – look to your own resources. I have scarcely enough men to defend Rome."

It was the answer Aurelius had expected. But Aetius continued. "If we win the battle tomorrow, the *I Britannicus* will be a battle-hardened legion, and what is more, a legion of citizens, and with that you can reconquer Britannia without my help."

"Thank you," said Aurelius, feeling his confidence return. "Now, if you will excuse me, I must hold my own council or war."

As he was leaving the tent, Aetius called after him: "Remember, the main thing is to stand firm. If your men hold the line, Attila's horse archers can do little to harm them, but if they break, they will be swept away like dust!"

Aurelius had got the message. All he had to do now was to hammer it into the heads of his own commanders. His council consisted of Uther, his tribunes and his *primus pilus*,[15] Publius. He told them everything he had learned from Aetius, then went on to make his own dispositions. "The first cohort will hold the front line. They must take one javelin and one spear. They must throw their javelins at the word of command, but on no account must they throw their spears – they are to kneel behind their shields and point their spears to hold off the horses and protect the archers in the second rank, just like we practiced on the parade ground. I wish we had more archers, but those we have are excellent. The Second Cohort must be ready to fill gaps in the front rank – remember what Aetius said – we must hold the line at any cost. The Third Cohort will strengthen our left flank – just in case the Alans turn tail. I will hold the cavalry in reserve for the final pursuit."

"Why not put the archers in the front rank?" said Uther.

"Because the Huns will pick them off as easily as shooting rats in a barrel. Our archers need to shoot from behind the shieldwall of the first rank."

Many other questions followed, and it was long past midnight before the council was at an end. Aurelius thanked his men and sent them to get some sleep, though in his own case, he felt that sleep would be impossible.

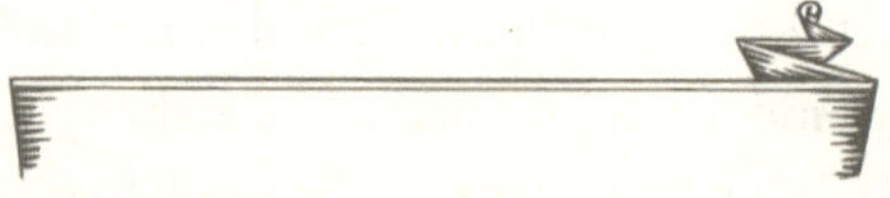

The Empire Strikes Back

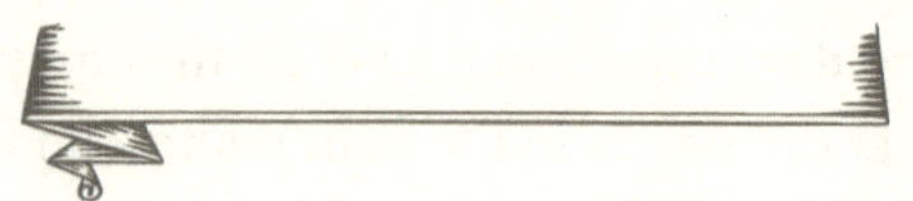

It was a short march to the Campi Catalaunici, and as Aetius had predicted, the Huns were waiting for them, their immense army seeming to spread across the whole horizon. After some skillful manouvring accompanied by some minor skirmishes, Aetius gained the advantage of an area of rising ground. Aurelius led his men onto a level plain just to his left, and the Alans formed up on his left. In the distance he could see the Visigoths under Theodoric and Waldere taking up their position on the right wing, reinforced by Gunther's Franks under Hagen's command. He had never seen so many men, and estimated that there must be at least 30,000 on Aetius side, though the number of Huns seemed countless as grains of sand – the rumours said 700,000. It was probably less, but they were certainly outnumbered. Aetius' legionaries were identifiable by their round blue *parma*[16] shields bearing a white imperial eagle, and by the steely glitter of their ridge helmets. Further back, on his flanks, Aetius had ranged the allies who were fighting with him. Their ranks were ragged, and their arms and armour a mixed bag: tunics of every colour, shields of different sizes, and a varied assortment of weapons. On his left flank were the Alans, who had drawn themselves up in a long line behind their shields. Each man was armed with whatever he had managed to acquire in a lifetime of fighting, though there was a general similarity in their small, round, wooden shields, and long slashing swords. It was hard to see Theodoric's Visigoths and Waldere's Aquitani clearly, but they presented a similar spectacle to the Alans, except, perhaps, that the constellation of metallic glints that shone through the morning mist suggested that they were better armed.

Aurelius felt proud of the turnout of his own army, their dragon shields giving them a unified look. However, he was under no illusions. Though they looked outwardly similar to Aetius' men, they were greatly inferior as a fighting force. Indeed, they were probably the only men on the battlefield who had no experience of an actual battle.

He rode along the ranks to ensure that the dispositions were as he had ordered, speaking words of encouragement to the men as he went. When he reached the front rank, he was particularly emphatic: "Remember, your job is to protect the archers. When the Huns attack, throw your javelins, then kneel behind your shields and hold out your spears. Archers, aim for the horses! Hold the line! If you hold the line, the Huns cannot break you! You must hold the line!"

But the men seemed restless, and their composure was shaken by a horrified whisper that ran along their ranks: "Attila!"

Aurelius repeated his message: "Have no fear. Just hold the line!"

Then a soldier called out: "Attila – there he is! Right opposite us! Why do *we* have to fight him! Aetius should do that!"

Aurelius followed the man's stare, and he saw a man on horseback who seemed to be the leader of the Hunnic horde. They were no more than 500 paces away and were trotting slowly forward, awaiting the command to charge. It was too far to see many details, but he picked out a well-armoured man who was waving a sword above his head. His heart jumped – The Sword of Tengri! The Huns gave a great cheer when they saw the sword, and Aurelius was reminded once again of the power of a symbol. If only this battle were over and he was waving his own Sword of Albion!

Attila swung the sword down, and his hosts charged. As the distance shortened, Aurelius could see for the first time what the Huns really looked like . He was appalled at their ghastly appearance, their strange Asiatic features which led some to attribute their origin to the union of their women with evil spirits of the wilderness, and their even stranger way of dressing – in furs and animal skins. His blood ran cold. This was not what Aetius had told him! It looked as though his untrained legion would have to face the mightiest warriors on earth, while the experienced Romans and Visigoths looked on. Perhaps this was what Aetius intended all along, thought Aurelius bitterly. Let Attila weaken himself by his attack on the unimportant Armoricans and Alans in the centre, then close in on both sides and finish him off.

He galloped back to tell the bad news to Uther, but he had hardly time to splutter it out, when the Huns had reached his front ranks. They attacked in wheeling movements, riding up to the lines, discharging their arrows, then suddenly turning back again. The front line immediately began to break with shouts and screams of agony. Some men fell back, others, enraged, stepped forward and threw their spears, leaving themselves defenseless to the next wave of attack. They tried to hide behind their shields, but the line was broken, leaving them vulnerable to the arrow storm. They fell like grass under the scythe, and in minutes, Aurelius' front line was a line no longer, but a seething mass of tortured humanity, and the red dragon shields that Aurelius had been so proud of were rendered unrecognisable by new, hideous patterns of blood.

He looked on with horror and pity. He had trained them as best as he knew how, but they had never expect an onslaught like this – by the most fearsome horse archers in the world. Their reputation, strange appearance and lightening speed filled Aurelius' men with superstitious dread and they forgot their training and acted like frightened children. He wished he had done more to prepare them, but there was no time to waste on regrets. He had to do his best to remedy the situation.

"Second Cohort!" he ordered in a choked voice – not that the tone of his voice mattered. It was a horn that sounded the order. But nothing happened. "Uther!" he shouted. "Take my bodyguard and lead the Second Cohort into the line!" Aurelius watched the command being relayed, and his legionaries slowly manouvre into place. It was frustrating to watch – it was all too slow! The next attack would break through and the centre would be lost. But to his astonishment and relief, the next attack never came. The tide of Huns surged past his front and onto Aetius' position. He breathed a sigh of relief, and not just because his legion was spared. Things were beginning to work out as Aetius had predicted. He had not been Aetius' dupe after all. It seemed foolish now that he had ever thought such a thing. A moment later, Uther was back at his side again. "Second Cohort in position."

"Let's hope they learn from the mistakes of the First," said Aurelius grimly, but though the attacks continued, they were less determined. It was clear that Attila was concentrating his main strength on Aetius.

"Look!" said Aurelius, seeing movement in Aetius' lines. "That is how it should be done!"

Aetius' army may have lacked Roman legionaries, but the auxiliaries who made up the bulk of its numbers were well trained and had long experience. The maniples and cohorts seemed to move like pieces on a chessboard, and their lines were always straight. They were arranged in blocks with a space between each block. This allowed the ranks behind to march through unimpeded, and bring new strength into the fight. When a man fell, another took his place. No man surged forward too eagerly, or hung back too fearfully; they all pressed on together as steadily and mechanically as if it were a training exercise. The waves of Huns seemed to break against them and fall back like breakers that crash onto the beach and slide back harmlessly into the ocean.

For a while, the battle seemed to hang in the balance, and then a trumpet call signalled the front rank to open gaps, and a sixty ballistae spat forth their bolts of death. Their impact on massed horse archers was devastating as the bolts were capable of passing through several horses one after another. Men screamed, horses whinnied and the grass turned red.

"You see, Uther. Artillery!" For some reason, the sight of the carnage produced by the ballistae made Aurelius feel exultant. It was perhaps because all his theories about battle were being proved correct – an army must have archers, artillery, cavalry. All of which his own army still lacked in sufficient numbers, despite his efforts.

His attention was drawn back to his own legion by Uther, who cried exultantly: "Our line is holding!" It appeared that the Second Cohort had seen with horror the errors of the first, and were hanging on to their spears for dear life, with the result that the waves of horse archers did not dare to come close. Best of all, they had remembered to kneel and the archers were at last brought into play. This was enough to ward off the mounted attacks, and the Huns regrouped to try another strategy.

"They're dismounting!" said Uther, noticing a sudden change in the rhythm of the battle.

"Infantry attack! Bring up the Third Cohort!" ordered Aurelius. A horn sounded the order, and this time the men responded, though not fast enough, or in good enough order. The front line was already under pressure by the time they were in a position to reinforce it. The line wavered under the murderous onslaught, but whenever a man fell, he was replaced by a fresh soldier from the Third Cohort. How Aurelius wished his men had the level of discipline that would enable an entire rank to replace another! Nevertheless, his men were fighting well, remembering to keep their shields close together and to stab at the enemies' faces from over the tops of the shields. They were learning that the Huns were more bark than bite. Their epilapid eyes gave them an alien look, and their outlandish way of dressing added to the effect, but they were generally smaller in stature than the average Armorican. Also, the light *urepos* was ill-suited to the cut and thrust of infantry combat. The Roman *spatha* was a much more useful weapon. It had a longer reach and could be used just as effectively for stabbing, or slashing.

"They're still holding!" cried Uther, "and strongly too!"

Satisfied that his own part of the battle was going well, Aurelius surveyed the battlefield. The fighting on Aetius' flank continued, though it was clear that the Romans were getting the best of it. The Visigoths were doing well too. Waldere was making good use of the Dragon's Mouth tactic, as was Theodoric further along the line, and their dragons were gobbling up the enemy 30 at a time. Seeing this, the Huns stopped their head on attacks and began sweeping across their front, releasing their arrows then whirling out of range. Waldere had a riposte to this, too. He sent out "stingers" – rows of men who knelt behind their shields while holding their spears forwards. This caused the Hunnic horses to veer or baulk, as a horse will never charge onto a spear point. Theodoric attempted the same tactic, though with less success.

Seeing that his Huns were making no progress against the Visigoths, Attila ordered his Ostrogoths forward, in the hope that their similar Nordic style of fighting would make an impact on the resilient Visigoth lines. The Ostrogoths strode forwards on foot, their shields held in a shieldwall before them, threw their spears, then charged the Visigoth lines with visible effect. Waldere's Aquitani staggered under the impact and began to give ground. Theodoric's Visigoths fared just as badly. They suffered heavily under the spear shower. A spear has a shorter range than an arrow, but it is a much heavier weapon and can pierce both shield and body armour. When the Ostrogoths charged, the Visigoths broke, and a rumour was whispered down the line that Theodoric and been struck down by a Hunnic spear.

Aurelius shook his head sadly as he reflected that this was a result of their tradition that their leader must be at the forefront of battle, and, no doubt, Theodoric had been striving to fulfil his boast – all the barbarians were the same, the Alans, the Ostrogoths – and Attila himself. How much wiser was the Roman tradition of a leader who fought with his mind; who chose a place where he could survey the battle, and sent orders with messengers and trumpet calls. Even now, the results of this foolish tradition were playing out before him. The Visigoths seemed to crumple visibly as the terrible news spread among their ranks, and their position was pushed back by a fresh wave of Hunnic horse archers, taking advantage of the situation. Seeing this, cries went up from the Alan contingent. They feared that they would be rounded upon by the Huns, and they too began to retreat.

Aurelius' heart sank. This looked like a turning point in the battle, and he felt he had to do something to save the day. If the Alans turned tail, his own flank would be exposed to the Huns, and his precious legion would be wiped out after all. He sent an order to his *equites* but nothing happened. Had the messenger been killed? Did the tribune doubt the order? He could stand the frustration no longer, and immediately contradicted his own reflections of a moment ago by spurring *Achilles* towards his equites, and leading them himself towards the Alan lines. He was thankful now that he had joined the men in their training, though every one of them had more experience in the saddle than he. He had no lance, so he drew his sword and shouted the command to charge. They raced across the place where the Alan front line had been, heading for the enemy's flank. Aurelius should have been filled with fear. He was no cavalryman, and he was heading an attack into the best horse archers in the world. Yet he felt a thrill of elation; the heavy weight of responsibility for his legion evaporated like mist, and there was only himself and his horse flying through a pure Elysium.

The Huns saw their peril and wheeled their horses to meet the attack. But Aurelius felt no fear, rather he marvelled at their skill. It seemed that horse and man were one and that it was not men he was fighting, but some kind of centaur beast from the old legends. But despite their skill on horseback, the Huns were hampered by their numbers, and too few were able to turn. Those that could, galloped forward, and unleashed a volley of arrows. Aurelius felt the whoosh of air as they flashed past him, but they clattered on his cuirass and bounced off, or stuck in his shield, which soon began to look like a hedgehog. Their racing horses closed the gap in seconds, and the danger of arrows was over. The Huns were now at a disadvantage. Both horses and men were smaller than those Aurelius led. What is more, they wore no armour and carried no lance. They drew their swords, but they lacked the reach of a lance. The only advantage they had – their superior horsemanship – was of little use to them in such a melee. The first Hun that Aurelius encountered was bowled over by the weight and speed of *Achilles*. The next swiped at him with his urepos, but Aurelius caught the blow on his shield, and stabbed him in the chest with his long-reaching spatha. The man screamed and fell from his horse. It was the first man Aurelius had killed, but he had no time to think about it, as Huns were attacking him on both sides. He hacked blindly with his spatha not seeing or caring where the blows landed, and cleared a path before him like a man who scythes wheat. He received many blows in return, but his excellent armour warded them off. Then, in what seemed like no time at all, there was no enemy in front – he had led his men straight through their ranks, and in all that carnage, *Achilles* had never once let him down. The Huns might be one with their horses, but they mistreat them, and Aurelius realised that a man can be one with a horse in a different way – as friends who help each other. He patted *Achilles* in thanks, then wheeled for another charge, but the situation had changed. The Huns were now galloping in the opposite direction pursued by the Aquitani cavalry led by Waldere riding *Lion*, and holding *Mimming* high and waving it like a banner. Close behind them came the vast infantry of Visigoths led by Thorismund, Theodoric's son. Seeing this, Aurelius signalled to his men to hold back. They had turned the tide of the battle, and were not needed now. The Aquitani and Visigoths could finish it off.

Aurelius suddenly realised that he was exhausted. He pulled off his helmet and felt the cool breeze in his hair. He had lost his cloak, his cuirass was dented in several places and he had blood on his arm and on his left thigh. Although he had not realised it, he had received several wounds, fortunately, none of them severe. The light was failing, and it looked as though the battle was all but over. The Huns had taken refuge in their camp, which was fortified with wagons, and the Aquitani and Visigoths were trying to break in. Aurelius looked on, waiting for an opportunity to deploy his cavalry. Not far away, he could see his own front line waiting patiently for the next onslaught.

At last there was full darkness, and the sounds of battle were replaced by a kind of low hum – the moans and groans of the thousands of dead and dying. Aurelius led his cavalry back to his own lines, and gave the order to make camp, which meant building a defensive rampart. The men were exhausted and it was badly done, though better than nothing. Troops of the Third Cohort who had seen less of the action, were detailed to carry the wounded to a dressing station, and to stand guard in watches through the night. Aurelius had scarcely finished these arrangements, when a messenger came from Aetius. There was to be a council of war in the Visigoth camp. He delegated the post-battle arrangements to Uther, and made his way to the Visigoth camp with a unit of his bodyguard for protection. By then, the night was well worn, but a dim light came from a haze-clouded moon. That ghostly light revealed a scene from some hellish otherworld. Everywhere, men lay dead and dying, suffering from the most terrible wounds. Disembodied arms and legs, bodies without heads, heads without bodies, bloody heaps that were once human lay in his path. The torn and bloodied rags, and the fragments of weapons and shields showed that they were representative of all the tribes who had fought that day. Visigoth lay beside Ostrogoth, an Alan embraced a Hun, and here was one of his own Armoricans whose body had not yet been brought in. The sight was sickening. He felt ashamed of himself for having played a part in it. Was anything worth all this suffering? The answer was obvious. It was not. He resolved there and then that when he got back to Armorica, he would give up his pretentions to the throne of Britannia and return to the monastery. But no! It could not be.

His brother would only take up the baton and carry out the plan of reconquest which would bring the same kind of suffering to his own beloved country. His heart was filled with gloom when he entered Aetius' tent, but Aetius seemed as unaffected as if he had spent a day on the training ground.

"Welcome Aurelius! Still with us, I see. Well, we have had a good day of it, thanks to Waldere. It is not an exaggeration to say that he saved the day."

Aurelius looked up with surprise. He was under the impression that he and his Armorican cavalry had saved the day, but he was too proud to say so. Waldere bowed to acknowledge the compliment. He looked tired and drawn, but he was not too tired to say, "Thorismund was not far behind me, and the Armorican cavalry played a part."

Aurelius gave a slight bow in acknowledgment. In any case, what did it matter who had played the best part in the slaughter? He was finished with all that! Aetius noticed his confusion, and realised that Aurelius still did not know exactly what had happened. So he explained that, when Theodoric had been killed, the Visigoths had lost heart, but Waldere managed to rally his Aquitani in a renewed attack. Inspired by his lead, Thorismund had rallied the Visigoths, and together they had turned the tide of the battle. He acknowledged Aurelius' part in heading off the Huns, but explained that the decisive action was Waldere's counter-attack, which went all the way to Attila's camp, and would have finished him off, had it not been for the fortifications.

Aurelius thanked him for the explanation, but cared little whether it had been he or Waldere who had saved the day. All the twists and turns of the battle flashed through his mind, and he realised that there had been many moments when it could have gone the other way and wiped out his precious legion – and himself for that matter!

Words of heated argument broke into his private reflections. It seemed that Aetius had no plans to renew the battle and his allies were objecting.

"But he is beaten!" protested Waldere. "His horse archers are useless in defence, believe me, I know that from experience! We can storm his camp and finish the job in a few hours!"

Aetius looked sternly at Waldere. "I understand your eagerness to finish the job. I know your zeal from that lay about you! We all want to finish Attila, but we have to see the bigger picture: what will be the price of victory, and will it be what we Romans call a Pyrrhic victory?"

Waldere didn't know the term, but he guessed what Aurelius was getting at. Sangiban, on the other hand, had no idea what he was talking about and it showed in his puzzled expression, as did several of the other leaders. Seeing this Aetius spelled it out: "Attila is broken. His westward march has been stopped. What can he do now but retreat? It is true that he may attack the west next year, but the myth of his invincibility is discredited. Did you know that his fabled sword, The Sword of Tengri, was broken in the battle? That will undermine the loyalty of his followers. He will never be a serious threat again. Also, I do not wish to risk my legion – probably the last legion that Rome will ever field – or the armies of this alliance, in a desperate attack on a fortified position. Of course, we will win – but at what cost? If my army – Rome's last legion – is decimated, Rome will be a victim of the next petty tyrant to cross the Rhine."

There were grunts of agreement. Everyone present was battle weary, and few relished the thought of renewing the conflict the next day. Even Waldere was content to accept Aetius' decision. The only one to object was Thorismund. "My lord, it is my duty under the Visigoth code of honour to avenge my dead father. I say we fight on!"

"He is avenged," said Aetius, "in every Ostrogoth you killed in your onslaught, and if I were you, I would watch my back."

Thorismund bridled, suspecting an insult, but Aetius' explanation made him see sense. "My father was a Goth and I know very well that Gothic kings are chosen by election. You have brothers in Regnum

Gothorum who, as soon as they hear of Theodoric's death, will be making their claim to the crown."

Those words put the matter in a different light, and Thorismund was as eager as the others to leave.

"First we must see Attila off," said Aetius. "My guess is that he will make his way back to Pannonia to lick his wounds. I doubt that he'll bother us again."

As the kings and lords were leaving, Aetius once again asked Aurelius to stay behind. When they were alone, he said, "What do you really think, Aurelius?"

"I understand what you said about preserving the last Roman legion, but surely we could have finished the job without such terrible losses..." He hesitated, then went on. "There must be another reason – a private one, something that you could not tell to the other allies."

Aetius gave an ironic laugh. "You are very perceptive Aurelius! There is indeed another reason, and it is this: a Roman general cannot afford to be too successful – look what happened to Stilicho! I very much fear that Attila's end will herald my own. When he is dead, the emperor will have no further use for me, and..."

He indicated the cutting of his throat with a flick of his finger.

Aurelius was thoughtful as he made his way to his own camp. He had learned so many lessons in the past 48 hours: that battles are won or lost long before the combatants take to the field, that politics are even more important than battles, and that there is nothing more powerful than a symbol. Above all, he had proved his legion – and now he was ready to deploy it on what it was created for: to bring about the liberation of his lost realm – Britannia!

But that is not how it turned out. Despite Uther's urging, Aurelius, on the advice of King Aldroenus, and the support of the Armorican council, judged it wise to keep the legion in Armorica as long as Attila was at large.

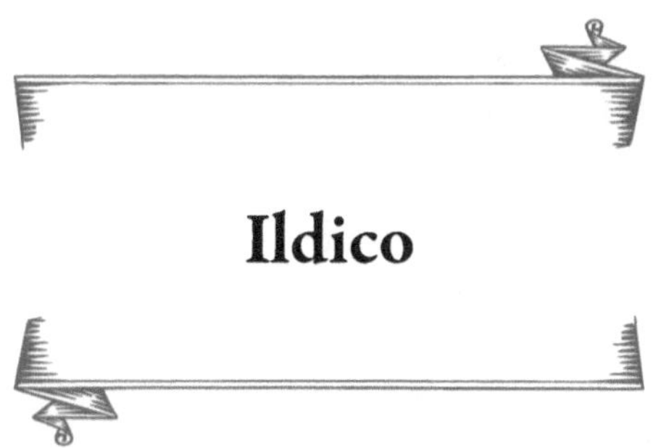

Ildico

When Attila got back to Etseliri he needed consolation, and he chose – Hildaz. He had been saving the most beautiful woman in Pannonia as a reward for a faithful servant, but they had all let him down – all! So he might as well take her himself. Hildaz was delighted. Now at last her beauty had its rightful reward. It mattered little that Attila was as ugly as a Hunnic horse, with a large head, a barrel chest and short legs, because he was – Attila – the most powerful male among powerful males.

She approached him in bed with the humility she had been taught. Crawling up from the foot of the bed, worshipping his manhood with her mouth, then turning over and offering her body to his delight. He took her roughly, enjoying her screams of pain as he tore into her virgin flesh, and the way she writhed, at first in pain, and then in delight. But the warrior in him would have preferred to have skewered an enemy – Aetius, perhaps – and seen him writhe in agony as he thrust his urepos into his guts.

He was determined to fight back; to try again to take the whole of Gallia and Hispania, and he saw the Ostrogoths as an important part of his plan. They had fought well at the Campi Catalaunici and he wished to cement the alliance. And that was how Hildaz had her nose pushed out before she had got it in: Attila's envoys arranged a marriage with an Ostrogoth princess called Ildico. Not only was she an important political pawn, but she was beautiful in the way that only an Ostrogoth can be: her hair was as golden as the sun, and she was golden everywhere: on her head, under her arms and in a golden triangle between her legs. Her eyes were as blue as the sky on a summer's day, and her skin was a creamy white, like milk, her full breasts tipped with pink nipples – a delicious desert of strawberries and cream! The most beautiful woman of the Huns seemed plain by comparison, with her black eyes, dun coloured skin and brown nipples, and as a result, Hildaz found herself in the women's quarters with all Attila's former wives, neglected and frustrated.

On the night of the wedding feast Attila undressed and lay in bed waiting for Ildico to crawl from the bottom of the bed and worship his manhood – but she shuffled off her clothes and slipped in beside him.

"That is not the way we Huns do these things," said Attila. "You should crawl respectfully from the foot of the bed."

"I am not a Hun," said Ildico, proudly. "We Ostrogoth women are respected by our husbands."

Attila felt a flash of anger, but it was assuaged by Ildico's loveliness, and by a sense that her demand for respect increased her value. "Do Ostrogoth women know how to..." he finished the sentence with a coarse word in Hunnic.

"I'll show you," she said. "Suckle my teats first, and then I'll suck you!"

He was not used to being told what to do by a woman, but when it was to do something so delicious, how could he refuse? He took an ample teat into his mouth and began to suckle it while fondling the other. Then he switched sides – but what was that taste? Just the taste of an Ostrogoth woman, perhaps.

But it wasn't. It was the taste of poison, and the morning after their wedding feast, Attila was found dead in his bed, with Ildico weeping by his side.

"Murder!" some shouted.

Ildico sobbed all the more and protested her innocence, and Attila's physicians could find no mark upon his body, nor any of the usual signs of poison; though it didn't really matter, because Ildico would have to die anyway.

Attila's body was placed in the midst of a plain and lay in state in a silken tent where his lords might pay tribute. The best horsemen of the entire tribe of the Huns rode around in circles, and sang of his deeds in a funeral dirge: "The chief of the Huns, King Attila, descendant of the Great Nimrod. Nurtured in Engaddi. By the grace of Tengri, King of the Huns, the Goths, the Danes and the Medes. The dread of the World; lord of bravest tribes, sole possessor of the Scythian and German realms; he captured cities and terrified both empires of the Roman world." Then they placed his body in a gold coffin and buried him with great riches in a secret vault. His wives were sent to accompany him to the realm of Tengri, among them, his first wife, Kreka, Ospirin, Hildaz and Ildico. The thralls who prepared the grave were all slain so that no grave robbers could desecrate the great man's tomb.

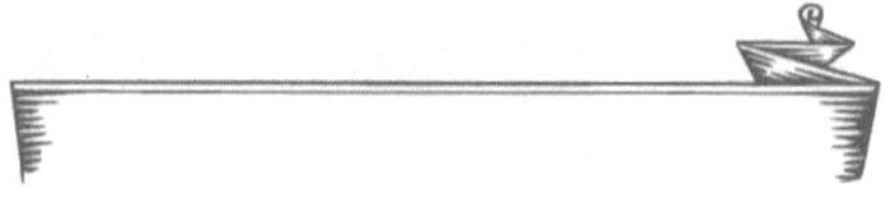

Grand Alliance

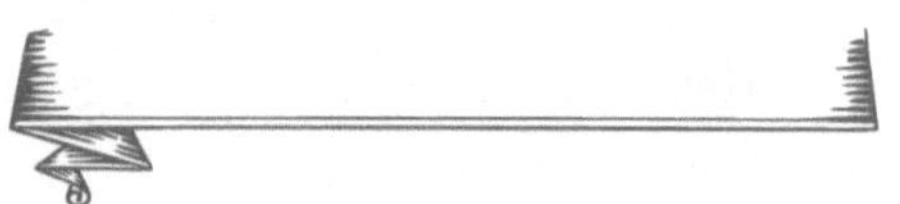

For the first time in many years, Armorica was safe, and Aurelius and Uther could revive their long cherished plan – to reconquer Britannia! But not everyone supported that plan. Judocus, whose political power had grown while Aurelius and Uther had been concerned with military matters, was a strong advocate of disbanding the legion, and for good reasons too: the cost of supporting it was ruinous, and while people had been willing to pay the necessary taxes when the country was in peril, they baulked at the idea of supporting 3,000 men in idleness. As for reconquering Britannia, it seemed more and more like a fool's dream. It is true that a large proportion of the population of Armorica were exiles from Britannia – but that was a long time ago, and all they wanted to do now was to live their lives in peace, free from burdensome taxes.

Judocus was not a bad man, and he was not opposing Aurelius for the sake of his own aggrandisement, but with a genuine concern for the people of Armorica. King Aldroenus, though less involved in politics in his declining years, shared that concern, to the extent that he took it upon himself to speak to Aurelius personally: "Attila is dead, his sons are defeated, and there is no threat to the kingdom, so it is time to decommission your legion. Keep 300 men for the defence of Riedonum[17] and send the rest back to their farms. They can be summoned as levies if the need arises."

"But what about...?"

The old king gave a sad smile. "...Britannia? It is a bear-pit now, is it not? Ravaged by Picts and Scots, Angles and Saxons, and every other raider who is looking for easy pickings. Would you send our Armorican youth into a bear-pit?"

"I am Britannia's rightful king – and it is the rightful inheritance of a good many of our people; those who fled here when the Romans left."

Aldroenus shook his head. "Nevertheless, it is an impossible dream. Give it up and make the best of what you have here. I am old now and you will soon succeed me. You will make a good king, and the country is safe and can be wealthy again – if we do not waste our resources on – impossible dreams."

Aurelius felt his resolution weakening. Aldroenus' arguments were strong, but on top of that his experience of battle, the needless slaughter, the waste of life, had given him a distaste for arms. He was tempted to resign the succession to Uther and rejoin the monastery, but his sense of duty wouldn't let him – and what about his duty to the people of Britannia, suffering the depredations of the tyrant Vortigern, and the numerous raiders? What should he do? How should he act?

In the end, he decided to follow Aldroenus' advice and disband the legion. He would improve on Judocus' plan, though. In addition to keeping 300 professional legionaries, he would make an alliance with his old friend, Waldere, so that, in the event of attack, he would have much larger forces to draw upon.

Uther was devastated at the news. "After all we've been through! All that work building up the legion, battling with devil himself and saving Aetius from disaster!"

"I'm sorry, Uther, but look at it like this: our legion, alongside Aetius and his foederati, saved civilization, so our work was not wasted – far from it!"

"And now it is a well-honed fighting machine. It is now or never."

Aurelius breathed a heavy sigh. "Let it be never! I never want to see again what I saw on the Catalaunian Plains the day after the battle! The

Huns are history and we have peace, and I want to make the most of it!"

"You can only enjoy peace when you are strong! With only 300 men we will be a target for every would-be imperialist, whether he be Roman or barbarian!" protested Uther.

"We are safe enough here at the end of the world," said Aurelius.

"The Romans thought it worth conquering, and no doubt Attila would have found his way here soon enough had it not been for our legion."

"Had it not been for Aetus' field army!" corrected Aurelius. "It is true that we played an important part, but let's not exaggerate!"

The brothers couldn't agree, but on the following day, they received news that changed everything.

"Aetius is dead!" said the messenger. He went on to describe how the emperor Valentinian had personally killed Aetius by slashing his throat, and how a patrician called Petronius Maximus had engineered it by egging him on. Soon after, Maximus persuaded two of Aetius' commanders, Optilia and Thraustila, to revenge him by assassinating Valentinian. There was no obvious successor to the throne, and the Roman world was in chaos. "And the latest news is that the Vandals are planning an attack on Italia," concluded the messenger.

"That means every warlord in Gallia will join in the struggle for power," said Uther. "Do you still want to disband our legion?"

Aurelius was devastated to hear that his former commander, Aetius had died in at the hand of the very man he had fought to protect, and unsettled that it was just as he had predicted. The only consolation, though a small one, was that Uther's beloved legion had been spared. As for himself, his only thought was to do the best thing for his country, and his idea about an alliance with the Aquitani seemed more important than ever.

Aurelius arrived in Aquitania to find that King Ælfhere had died and that Waldere had succeeded him. He was already respected as a good king, made wise by his wide experience, his suffering, and the good advice of his beloved Hildegund, and was, at that moment, trying to decide what to do about the latest news from Rome.

He was delighted to see his old friend and companion in arms, and the idea of an alliance was welcomed as soon as it was proposed, the only matter for debate was who else they could persuade to join them. Waldere had the grand idea of a grand alliance of nations stretching from Aquitania to Armorica to include all of the eastern seaboard of Gallia, and they spent most of the day discussing how they could bring it about.

That evening, at the welcome feast, they relived some of the highs and lows of the battle with Attila.

"I really thought I'd turned the battle!" said Aurelius with a wry laugh.

"That's nothing," said Waldere, "I really thought I'd lost it. You see, when the Ostrogoths attacked, the heart went out of us. They are kin after all. Our sagas tell how the Goths left Gothland and wandered the world until they finally settled in Gallia, one group in the east – the Ostrogoths, and one group in the west – the Visigoths. But that battle made us feel like we were reliving the *Hildebrandslied* in which father and son fight each other. We gave ground at first – but what choice had we? We rallied..."

"*You* rallied? I thought it was...but never mind..."

"Yes, when I saw the Huns pouring into the breach, I felt I had a real enemy to fight."

"And you carried the fight to Attila."

"Yes, with the help of Thorismund, and we would have finished him off had it not been for Aetius."

Waldere was thoughtful for a moment. "There is an interesting twist to that story that perhaps you have not heard. The Ostrogoths felt just as bad about attacking us, though they had no choice with Attila at their backs – I know what that feels like! So they were determined to be rid of him. They sent a beautiful young woman called Ildico to cement their alliance in marriage, but with a secret mission to poison him – and she succeeded, brave girl, at the cost of her life. They are a free people now, and we are allies again."

"It's a good story," said Aurelius, "she should be celebrated in one of your sagas."

"Yes. She was another scyldmæden."

"Or Amazon."

"There was a woman involved in the death of Aetius, too. Have you heard that tale?"

"Only that Valentinian killed him with his own hand."

"He was egged on by Maximus – and for good reason too. You see, Valentinian had seduced – some said 'raped' – his beautiful wife, Licinia, and he wanted revenge. However, he knew that he couldn't get at Valentinian while Aetius was still around, so he criticised Aetius to the extent that Valentinian was persuaded to kill him, then, with Aetius out of the way, he set on Optilia and Thraustila to assassinate Valentinian."

"That's a mixed up tale!"

"There's more. Licinia's daughter, Eudocia, was engaged to Huneric, the son of the Vandal king, Geiseric, and Maximus cancelled the engagement – so now Geiseric is preparing for the invasion of Italia."

"Then we'd better get to work on that grand alliance we spoke of earlier."

"Yes, and you will have to call of your planned invasion."

"I'd already decided to do that. I was planning to disband my legion and make do with 300 professional warriors supported by levies – but if the chance comes again I might revive the idea, and I hope you'll give me your support. You see, with more men, there will be less killing.

Indeed, the very news of such a mighty army might terrify my enemies into surrendering without a fight."

Waldere shook his head decidedly. "I explained how the Visigoths and Ostrogths are kin, well, the Angles and Saxons are also kin, and we will not fight them."

He saw the disappointed expression in Aurelius' face and regretted that he had expressed himself so firmly, but an idea occurred to him: "You said that 300 professional warriors would be enough to protect Armorica. Well, I will send you those warriors, and in the event of an attack, will send the rest of my army. That means you can take your entire legion, plus all the levies you can raise, to Britannia. It is almost as good as if my army joined you."

Aurelius clapped him on the shoulder. "I owe you a great debt, and be assured, if my legion can ever be of assistance to you, it is at your service. We are hereditary enemies, I suppose; I a Celt and a Roman citizen, and you a Northman and – excuse the word – a barbarian. But I trust that we are firm friends!"

"Spare me the 'barbarian'! I enjoy the Roman baths as much as you do, and if only we had the knowhow to repair the aqueduct I would be in them every day! But yes, we are friends! We have faced the greatest trial together and come through. Are there any baths in Britannia, by the way?

"Plenty, and the best at Aquae Sulis. But returning there is still a dream and will probably never happen."

"Dream on! There was a time when I was held hostage by the most powerful man in the world, and the prospect of marrying my beloved Hildegund and ruling my beloved country seemed as far away as the Evening Star – but here I am, and none the worse for it – apart from this..."

He gave a rueful wave of his hand-shaped glove.

"But I still have this..." Here he waved his left hand, "...and, of course, that far-famed sword *Mimming*."

Mention of *Mimming* made Aurelius think for a moment of his own far-famed sword – The Sword of Albion – but he still had to find it, and perhaps that was just another impossible dream.

Historical Note

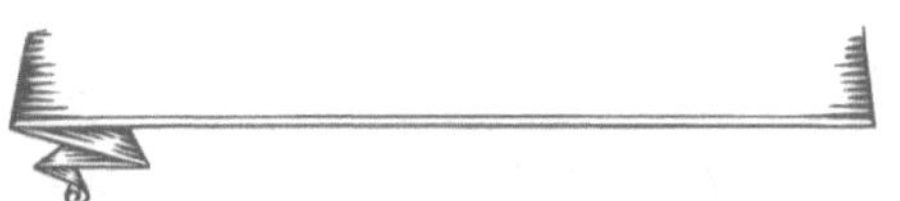

This book is based in part on my version of *Waldere* (2012). All that remains of this Anglo-Saxon epic are two short fragments found in 1860 by Professor Werlauff of the Royal Library, Copenhagen in the binding of a book. Fortunately, a German epic in Latin, *Waltharius Manu Fortis (Walther of the Strong Hand)*, written by Ekkehard of St Gall (d. 973), enables us to put these fragments in context, telling the full story of Waldere from his time as a hostage with Attila to his fight with Hagen and Gunther. This book places them in an even broader context by imagining that Waldere joins Aetius, along with Aurelius, to fight against Attila at the Battle of the Catalaunian Plains. That battle marks one of only two definite dates (451) in the whole of the period covered by the *English Dawn* pentalogy. It is documented by Procopius (c. 500 – c. 560), and though there is no mention of Aurelius or Waldere taking part in the battle, he does mention that the Armoricans were involved. The first part of this book is, in essence, a prose version of the story of *Waltharius* using Anglicised names (and including the *Waldere* fragments.)

My book, *Waldere* (2012), includes a detailed introduction and a reconstruction of the lost Anglo-Saxon epic, written in a modern version of Anglo-Saxon poetic metre, and, like this book, using Anglicised names. Part of that version is given below, adapted to tell a complete story. It omits the first part of the epic in which Waldere is Attila's hostage along with Hagen and Hildegund, and summarises his battles with eight of Gunther's retainers. The remainder of the poem is given in full (with a slight change at the end). The *Waldere* fragments are italicized, though there is much debate about where exactly they fit into the story (see J B Himes, 2009, p. 55ff). I have adopted the simplest solution, with Gunther speaking in the second extract. The problem is that the description of the sword seems to refer to *Mimming* – unless Weland made two remarkable swords. However, the only other solution, outlined by Himes, would require a convoluted rewriting of this scene, for which there is no evidence.

> Waldere and Hildegund, hostages no more,
> fled from Attila as far as they could,
> reaching the crossing of the Rhine at Worms.
> Now at long last their fears left them;
> but Gunther had heard of their flight from the Huns
> with Attila's riches, and thought of enriching
> himself by recovering the enormous ransom
> paid by his father as fealty to Attila.
> Hagen pleaded with him to drop this plan
> as a dangerous venture, difficult to pull off;
> but greedy Gunther would not be gainsaid.
> With twelve of his hearth-troop, including Hagen
> he attacked Waldere, who was waiting for them
> in a defile of the Vosges which he had fortified.
> Hagen asked for the gold and the girl also,
> but Waldere tried to negotiate with him
> and made him an offer of 100 rings,
> and then 200 – but it wasn't enough.
> So he had no choice but to fight him off.
> Waldere's position was impregnable;
> a narrow defile where the one man
> at a time could attack him.
> And that's how they came, one after another:

Camalo, Kimo, Werinhard, Ekrivid
Hadawart, Partravid, Gerwit, Randlof –
but Waldere slew them one by one
in single combat with his strong hand,
and, when the three remaining warriors
attacked with a trident, he took them down
just as surely as he had slain the others.
Gunther and Hagen then tried trickery,
pretending to leave, but lying in wait.

The following day, Waldere left the defile.
They rode for a mile, and then the maiden
looking behind her, beheld two men
coming down the hill at a hurried pace.
White-faced with fear she spoke to Waldere:
"Our end has come if we can't get away!"
He said to Hildegund as soon as he saw them:
"In vain did my strong hand vanquish my enemies
if I should die at last and be dishonoured.
It is better to die bravely in battle,
than to lose our possession and escape alone,
but my spear is broken and my sword is blunt.
Then Hildegund said, "Take the sword, *Mimming*,
shut up till now in its shining sheath,
spoil of the Huns, spare it not,
use it savagely to save our lives!"
Hildegund's words heartened the hero.
"Surely, Weland's work will never weaken
with any man who can wield Mimming;
hard-edged sword. It felled many heroes,
blood-stained and blade-pierced.
Attila's best warrior, show your bravery!

*Do not despair! The day is come
when your wyrd will lead you,
either to loss of life, or lasting glory
among the men of Middle-earth.
Nor may I ever reproach you, my friend,
that I saw you shrink from the swordplay,
or flee to the fort, though many foes
hewed on your hauberk with hostile swords!
You always furthered the fight they began,
and sometimes too wildly sought for war,
to clash in contest, mortal combat,
with another man. Be mindful of honour,
of great deeds, while God is with you!
Don't worry about your blade: that bravest of weapons
was given to help us! Use it on Gunther
to beat down his boast; he sought this battle
and stirred up strife in spite of justice!
He refused the sword, the rings of gold,
and many treasures: now he must, ringless,
flee from this fight to find his lord,
hasten homeward, or here shall he die
if he should be foolish enough to fight!"*

Then Gunther, hearing these words in his hiding place,
stepped out to fight, and, swinging his sword,
he made his boast: *"No better sword
was ever made than this of mine!
I know that Theodric thought to send it
to Widia himself, with a wealth of treasure,
in gold and goods, gifts fit for a king!
That's how the son of Weland saved his lord,
the kinsman of Nithhad, from cruel straits,*

who journeyed fast from the giants' land."
Waldere spoke, the battle-brave warrior,
holding in his hand the help-in-battle:
"So, you believed, friend of the Burgundians,
that Hagen's prowess would prevail in warfare
and defeat me! Now take, if you dare,
from a battle-worn man, this grey byrnie!
Here on my shoulders is Ælfhere's heirloom,
of good workmanship and gold-adorned,
a blameless armour for an atheling to wear
if only his hands help it out
when fighting foes. It never fails me
when cruel enemies crowd upon me,
meet me with swords, as you seek to!
Yet only One can award the victory,
He is ready to help whatever is right!
Whoso hopes for help from the Holy One,
the Grace of God, will surely get it,
if his ways have earlier earned him that.
Then haughty heroes may have their reward,
and wield their wealth!" Then he said to Hildegund:
"Take *Lions'* reins and run to safety
to the nearby wood while I welcome these warriors
with Weland's work – no words are sharper!"

Gunther was wroth and ran towards him,
with his hearth-companion, Hagen, beside him,
hailing Waldere in his haughtiest manner:
"Foulest of foes, you will be foiled
of your deadly deeds, your den is far away;
the cave whence you came like a cunning wolf
to gnash your teeth and attack your prey!

Now you must fight in an open field
and you'll soon find out if that's as favourable!
You have tempted fate with a fee of treasure,
refusing flight, you must stay and fight!"
Waldere defied him; was deaf to his words,
and turned from him to the other, Hagen:
"I have words for you, Hagen. Wait awhile!
Why is my faithful friend now my foe?
Before, you embraced me; now, you attack me!
I admit, I had hoped for your hospitality,
returning from my exile, not your anger!
I even brought gifts to reward your good will!
To think that I said to myself many times:
I fear no harm while Hagen lives!
I beg you now by our boyhood games,
recover your senses – remember those games.
What happened to the harmony we had?
It was always strong, never knowing strife,
or the tantalising traps of temptation.
It made you forget your father's face,
and me forget my fatherland.
And what about the oath we affirmed so often?
I beseech you old friend, do not provoke battle!
Let us keep our pact of peace through the ages.
If you agree, I'll reward you with gold,
and you'll leave this place enriched with praise!
Hagen replied with these wrathful words:
"First you use force, then claim friendship.
You ended our pact when you picked a fight
and killed my comrades and my kinsmen
even though you knew that I was there!
I could bear the rest, but for one blow;

uniquely dear was the darling youth
whom you reaped with your reaping hook!
This is the deed that destroyed our pact,
and now I vow to seek for vengeance
for my nephew's death. Now deeds shall speak!
Either I shall die or do something memorable!
With that, he readied himself for battle,
as did Gunther, greedy for gold.
Waldere too, prepared his war-gear.
All three were waiting to ward off blows,
shaking in anticipation beneath their shields.
Then the two attacked together;
rushed at Waldere, wielding their swords
one on each side to hinder his swings.
He was like a bear bristling with rage,
surrounded by hounds in the hunt;
they fear his claws and dare not close.
It was in this way that the conflict went on
until the ninth hour. Trouble afflicted them;
the toil of battle, the burning sun,
the threat of danger, and the fear of death.
Then Waldere said these words to himself:
"If it carries on this way they will wear me out
Fortune must change or I must force it!"
Having said these words, Waldere attacked.
He shattered Gunther's shield with his famous sword,
and with one almighty and amazing blow,
cut off his leg leaving a stump of thigh.
Then Gunther fell at Waldere's feet.
His retainer, Hagen, was horrified to see it.
Waldere wielded his weapon again,
meaning to inflict the final wound,

but Hagen bent his helmeted head
to block the blow and bear the pain,
but the hero could not check his hand,
and Hagen's helm, an ancient heirloom,
though finely forged, flew apart
in a shower of shards which sparkled in the air.
Mimming too, that mighty blade,
work of Weland, was also shattered
When the hero saw his bladeless hilt,
he grew indignant and groaned with despair,
and despite its magnificent metalwork
cast it aside, careless of its value.
But when the hero extended his hand
Hagen saw his chance and hacked it off,
and so the hand of the hero fell;
a hand that once was hated by tyrants;
a hand that once held numerous trophies,
but the mighty man ignored misfortune,
and proudly bearing the pains of the flesh,
stuck the bloody stump into his shield-strap,
and held his half-sword in his unharmed hand,
taking his vengeance with sudden violence.
He hewed at Hagen and hacked out an eye,
sliced his lips and knocked out six teeth.

The battles was over when this business was done.
Each of the men was marked with battle.
There lay Waldere's hand, there lay Hagen's eye,
and there lay the leg of Gunther.
In the same way they divided the treasure.
The two sat together, the third was lying down,
and they wiped the river of red from the flowers.

Meanwhile Waldere called to the woman
and she bandaged each wound as her bridegroom ordered.
When this was done he asked for drink:
"Now fetch some wine, and offer it first
to Hagen, my friend, then hand it to me,
since I endured more than the others,
and then to Gunther, a great-spirited man,
though sluggish at first in the work of slaughter!
The daughter of Hereric heeded his words,
but although the Frank was parched with thirst,
he said to the woman: "Waldere is first.
He is braver than me and excels in battle."
Then the three men, unconquered in mind,
though battered of body and bleeding all over,
playfully joked and jested while drinking:
"Henceforth you will hunt many a hart,"
said Hagen, "and make many gloves with their hides,
but stuff your right glove to give the appearance
of a hand and hold Hildegund with the other."
Waldere replied, "Why are you boastful,
since you'll see everything with a sideways glance!
So hear me, Hagen, when you get home
make a poultice of milk to mend your wounds."
They renewed their pact with repeated pledge,
and lifting Gunther, who was in great pain,
they put him on a horse and went to their homelands.
Waldere was welcomed home with honour,
and rallied his people to fight Attila.

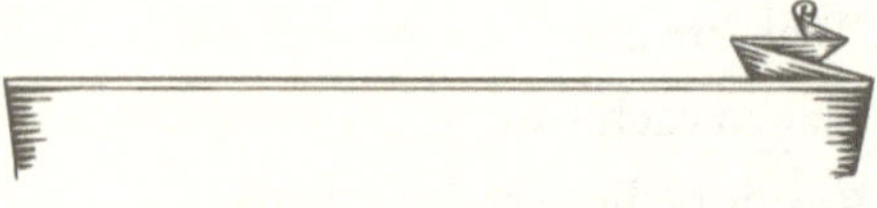

Bibliography

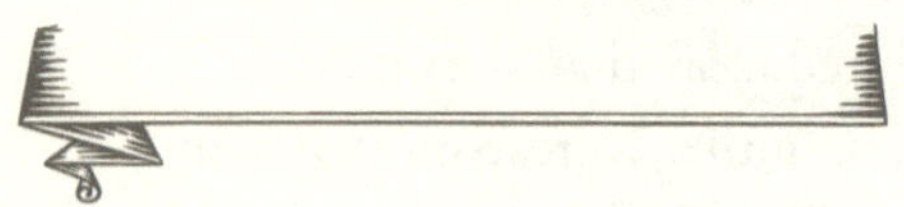

Andersson, Theodore M. *Die Oral-Formulaic Poetry im Germanischen*, in *Heldensage und Heldendichtung im Germanischen*, (ed.), Heinrich Beck, Berlin, De Gruyter, 1988.

Aurner, Nellie Slayton, *Hengest: a Study in Early English Hero Legend*. Iowa, University of Iowa Humanistic studies, 1873.

Chickering, Howell D., Jr. (trans.), *Beowulf: A Dual-Language Edition*. New York, Anchor Books, 1977.

Creasy, Edward Shepherd, *The Fifteen Decisive Battles of the World: from Marathon to Waterloo*. London, 1851.

Crowne, D. K., *The Hero on the Beach: An Example of Composition by Theme in Anglo-Saxon Poetry*, in *Neuphilologische Mitteilungen*, 61. Helsinki, University of Helsinki, 1960.

Evans, B. E., *The Life & Times of Hengest*. Ely, Anglo-Saxon Books, 2014.

Garmonsway, G. N. (ed.), *The Anglo-Saxon Chronicle*. New York, Dent, Dutton, 1972.

Gummere, Francis B., *The Oldest English Epic: Beowulf, Finnsburg, Waldere, Deor, Widsith, and the German Hildebrand, Translated in the Original Metres with Introduction and Notes* New York, 1923.

Heaney, Seamus (trans.), *Beowulf: A New Verse Translation.*

London, Faber and Faber, 1999.

Himes, Jonathan B., *The Old English Epic of Waldere,* Newcastle-upon-Tyne, 2009.

Jones, B., *An Atlas of Roman Britain*, Oxford, Oxbow Books, 1990.

Madden, Sir F., *Layamon's Brut, or Chronicle of Britain; a Poetical Paraphrase of the Brut of Wace.* London, Society of Antiquaries of London, 1847.

Magoun, F. P., *The Oral-Formulaic Character of Anglo-Saxon Narrative Poetry*, in *Speculum*, Vol 28, No. 3. Cambridge, MA, The Medieval Acadamy of America, 1953.

Morris, John, *The Age of Arthur.* London, Wiedenfeld and Nicolson, 1973.

Pace, Edwin, *The Long War for Britannia 367–644: Arthur and the History of Post-Roman Britain,* Pen & Sword Military, 2021.

Radice, Betty (ed.). Geoffrey of Monmouth: *The History of the Kings of Britain.* Harmondsworth, Penguin, 1966.

Sowerby, R, *Hengest and Horsa* in *Nottingham Medieval Sudies,* 51, 2007.

Stenton, Sir Frank M., *Anglo-Saxon England*. Oxford, OUP, 1973.

Tolkien, J. R. R., *Finn and Hengest*, reprinted in Bliss, Alan (ed.), *Finn and Hengest: The Fragment and the Episode*. London, Allen & Unwin, 1982.

Webster, C., *Hengest*, Leeds, East Keswick Press, 2012.

Webster, C., *Waldere*, Leeds, East Keswick Press, 2012.

[1] Bordeaux

[2] Chalon-sur-Saône

[3] baths

[4] an undead creature

[5] *as, assi* – a Roman bronze coin

[6] Roman mail armour

[7] Canterbury

[8] Brest

[9] Orleans

[10] mainly western Hungary/eastern Austria

[11] Troyes

[12] a plain near Châlons-en-Champagne

[13] general and nobleman

[14] general and king

[15] the senior centurion

[16] late Roman round shield

[17] Rennes

Did you love *Warrior*? Then you should read *Warrior Woman* by
Christopher Webster!

A tomboyish girl, fond of stories of shieldmaidens and waelcyries, gets
involved a viking raid led by her older brother. The raid goes wrong,
and her stepmother tries to teach her that her 'womanly weapons' have
more power. She goes on to seduce one king of Britannia and kill
another, thus playing as large a part in the conquest of that country
as her father, Hengest – but can she ever find true love? This is the
third part of the *English Dawn Pentalogy*, which tells the story of the
conquest and settlement of Britain by the Anglo-Saxons in the 5th
century, set against the broad sweep of events in the Dark Ages: the
decline of the Roman Empire, the rise of Attila the Hun, the raids by
the Picts and the Scots, and the usurpation of the kingship of Britannia
by the tyrant, Vortigern. These events are a prequel to the age of Arthur,

and the final chapter of the pentalogy sees Merlin setting up the sword in the stone for the king who is to come.

About the Author

Christopher Webster was brought up in Conisbrough, which is famous for its well-preserved castle. The castle and its link with Hengest provided the inspiration for this book. Another inspiration was studying English at university, particularly the study of Anglo-Saxon. His first publication was Poetry Through Humour and Horror. This was followed by many more educational publications including the best selling 100 Literacy Hours and study notes on Christina Rossetti and Ezra Pound. His writing about Conisbrough includes The Castle Trilogy, Coal Dust Kisses, four books of short stories and and Conisbrough Tales, which he describes as 'a Canterbury Tales' for Conisbrough. He also writes in other genres, such as Poetry, Regency Romance and Science Fiction under a range of pen-names. He is currently living in Laken and teaching in a European School.